WILD LIFE

ALSO BY CYNTHIA DeFELICE

CYNTHIA DeFELICE

WILD LIFE

SQUARE
FISH

Farrar Straus Giroux
New York

The author wishes to thank Terry Mcloud of the 680th Engineer Company, United States Army Reserves, Canandaigua, New York, for his kind and helpful input regarding overseas deployment of army reservists.

SQUARE
FISH

An Imprint of Macmillan
175 Fifth Avenue
New York, NY 10010
mackids.com

Square Fish and the Square Fish logo are trademarks of Macmillan and are used by Farrar Straus Giroux under license from Macmillan.

Square Fish books may be purchased for business or promotional use. For information on bulk purchases, please contact the Macmillan Corporate and Premium Sales Department at (800) 221-7945 x 5442 or by e-mail at specialmarkets@macmillan.com.

Library of Congress Cataloging-in-Publication Data
DeFelice, Cynthia C.
    Wild life / Cynthia DeFelice.
        p.   cm.
    Summary: When twelve-year-old Eric's parents are deployed to Iraq, he goes to live with grandparents he hardly knows in a small town in North Dakota, but his grandfather's hostility and the threat of losing the dog he has rescued are too much and Eric runs away.
    ISBN 978-1-250-03407-6 (paperback) / ISBN 978-1-4668-0111-0 (e-book)
    [1. Grandparents—Fiction.   2. Dogs—Fiction.
3. Runaways—Fiction.   4. Grief—Fiction.   5. Family life—
North Dakota—Fiction.   6. North Dakota—Fiction.]   I. Title.
PZ7.D3597Whl 2011   [Fic]—dc22   2010022531

Originally published in the United States by Farrar Straus Giroux
First Square Fish Edition: 2013
Book designed by Jay Colvin
Square Fish logo designed by Filomena Tuosto

5 7 9 10 8 6 4

AR: 5.0 / LEXILE: 860L

*To Buzz and Josie, and our adventures on
the North Dakota prairie*

WILD LIFE

1

I passed!" Erik Carlson flew through the back door and into the dark kitchen hollering, "Mom! Dad! I passed!"

The screen door slammed shut behind him, rattling the cups in the dish drainer, causing the cat to leap from his perch on the windowsill and head for cover in the pantry closet.

"Oh, Crenshaw, don't be such a scaredy-cat," Erik called over his shoulder as he ran through the room.

He liked Crenny well enough when she decided to sit on his lap and allow herself to be petted, but she wasn't nearly as much fun as his best friend Patrick's English setter, Hot Spots. Hot Spots was a champion bird dog. If she couldn't be hunting, she loved nothing more than hanging out with Patrick and Erik, fetching a ball or a stick, or learning just about any trick they felt like teaching her.

Crenshaw was named after one of Erik's father's favorite golf champions. Mr. Carlson didn't actually play golf, but he enjoyed watching it on television, something Erik just couldn't understand. Playing golf looked slow and boring enough. Watching it on TV, with the announcers speaking in hushed voices and sounding like they were spies discussing high-level national secrets, felt to him like torture. He enjoyed *doing* stuff, like building the tree fort he and Patrick were making in the woods behind Erik's house. He preferred games where he got to *move*; to run, swing a bat, toss a ball, or shoot something.

"Mom! Dad!" he called again. "Where are you guys?"

When there was no answer he went to the living room where his parents sat, Dad in his La-Z-Boy, Mom on the couch.

"Hey, what are you doing, sitting in the dark?" Without waiting for an answer, he flipped on the light switch and continued. "Guess what! I passed! I got the highest grade in the whole class, and Patrick got the second highest. We did better than the grownups, even!"

Erik and Patrick had been taking a New York State Hunter Safety course. He waved the certificate and held up a wallet-sized card. "See? It's official! Patrick and I can go hunting with his dad! Junior hunters can go out a week before opening day, and that's this coming weekend!"

He stopped for a second to catch his breath and noticed, for the first time, the strained smiles on his parents' faces.

There was a long pause before his mother said, "It's terrific you did so well in the course, honey."

"Congratulations, Erik," said Dad. "Let me see that."

Erik handed the certificate over, and an uneasy silence filled the room. He had the feeling that although his dad was looking at the piece of paper in his hands, he wasn't really seeing it. Erik's mother's eyes were on her lap, where her hands were balled into tight fists. The air felt heavy with things that weren't being said.

"What's going on?" Erik asked.

His parents looked at each other as if trying to decide who would answer, and the silence drew out even longer.

His mother sighed, and his dad placed the certificate carefully on the table beside his chair.

"We have something to tell you, Erik," said Dad.

His mother patted the cushion next to her on the couch. "Sit down."

Erik didn't want to sit down. He didn't like the sound of this at all. A terrible list of possibilities was running through his head: either his mother or father had contracted some horrible disease, or they were getting a divorce like his friend Mark's parents, or maybe it was Erik himself who had the disease. He had just had a physical for school. Maybe the doctors had found something . . .

"I might as well come right out with it," said his dad. "We've been called up. We're being deployed to Iraq."

Erik stared dumbly at his father.

"I know how you feel, honey," said his mom. "It came as a shock to us, too. We thought that, as reservists, well, we hoped this wouldn't happen. But the war's dragged on so long"—she shrugged helplessly—"and now we're needed."

Erik was having trouble believing his ears. His parents had been staff sergeants in the Army Reserves his entire life. To Erik, it was no big deal. They each reported for duty one weekend a month. They did drills and performed fitness exercises. They took classes to update the skills the Army had trained them for. Their specialty was training other soldiers and preparing them for duty.

And, while he'd always known that there was a chance his parents would be deployed, he—and they— had never really believed it would happen. They knew other reservists who, like his parents, had been in the Army thirty years or more and never been called up. Why his parents? Why now?

As he struggled to put his chaotic thoughts into words, his father went on. "We'll be training Iraqi soldiers and MPs so they'll be ready to take over when our military leaves. It's taking longer than expected to get the locals up to speed. Lots of guys have served several tours already. So"—he spread his hands—"it's our turn, buddy."

"But—*both* of you have to go?"

"It's unusual, but, well, we've got the training, and we're needed."

There were so many questions Erik wanted to ask. "What about your jobs?" His mom was a nurse and his dad was a mechanic at a Toyota dealership.

"The hospital's already been notified," said Mom. "And your dad told the guys at the garage today. They're not happy about losing us right now, but they know it's just the way it is. We'll have jobs when we come back, honey, don't worry about that."

"But—" Erik couldn't seem to stop saying that.

"It's all very sudden, I know," Mom said, reaching over to give his hand a squeeze.

"They try to give people more notice than this," Dad said. "But we serve at the need of the Army. They can't always keep up with changing demands. An order comes down, and it's got to be met."

"How long will you be gone?" Erik asked in a small voice.

"Six months is what they're telling us," said Dad. "But that could change. It could be longer."

Erik was quiet as the enormity of his parents' news began to sink in. Finally he forced himself to ask, "What about me?"

His parents exchanged a glance. "You know the Army requires us to have a family care plan," his mother said.

Erik vaguely remembered his parents talking to him about this, but it had been a long while ago and, at the time, it hadn't seemed important. "Yeah, I guess. But I forget what it is." He had a sudden thought. "Can I stay with Patrick?"

"No, hon—" Mom began, but Erik interrupted her.

"I bet his parents would let me! I could call right now and ask."

He took a step toward the phone, but his mom said, "Erik, no. I'm sure that Patrick's mother would be happy to have you. But you know she just had the new baby, and on top of that, they've taken in Patrick's grandmother, who requires a lot of Mrs. Holt's attention. It's just too much to ask right now. Especially for such a long time."

"We have to stick to our plan," said Dad. "I'm not sure we'd even be able to change it at this point. You'll be going out to stay with Oma and Big Darrell."

Oma and Big Darrell were his mother's parents, who lived in North Dakota. Erik couldn't believe his ears.

"But I don't even know them!"

"Oh, Erik, you remember when we went out to visit," said Mom.

"I was three years old! That was nine years ago! I don't remember anything about it, and I sure don't remember them."

"Well, you've spoken to them on the phone since then."

"Yeah, on Christmas and my birthday. 'Happy birthday. How's school? Goodbye.'"

9

"There's no need to be sarcastic." His mother looked at him pleadingly. "Honey, the Army wants you to be with family and so do we. Your father's parents have both passed on. There's no one else."

After a few beats of silence, Erik said sulkily, "I don't even know where North Dakota is." This was a slight exaggeration. He knew it was one of those big block-shaped states out west somewhere.

Dad got out the road atlas and opened it to the map that showed the whole United States. With his finger, Erik traced the route from upstate New York, where he lived, to Fortuna, North Dakota. "That's really far," he said glumly.

"Not as far as your mother and I are going," Dad answered, in a failed attempt to sound jolly.

"How am I going to get there?"

"You'll fly out."

"How long will *that* take?"

"All day."

"All day!" Erik turned to his mother for help. "Mom, I'll go nuts sitting in an airplane all day!"

"It will actually be three different airplanes, Erik. Company resource personnel looked into it today. Your flights are booked."

Erik groaned. "What if I get on the wrong plane

by mistake and end up in . . . in . . ." He paused, trying to think of a place more remote and less appealing than North Dakota, but couldn't come up with one.

"The airline people won't let you get lost," Mom said calmly.

Erik searched his brain for another argument. Then he had it! "What about school? There's no way I can be out of school for that long. I'll get way behind in everything."

"You don't need to worry about your schoolwork," Dad answered, as if that was Erik's actual concern. "Your grandmother will be enrolling you in school out there. And your records are being sent, so they'll know which classes to put you in."

"When do I—we—have to leave?"

"You leave on Friday," Mom said quietly. "Our flight leaves Saturday morning, and we want to take you to the airport and see you off."

2

Erik was stunned into speechlessness. His parents had said it was sudden. He'd heard them say the Army tried to give people more advance notice before they were deployed. But he'd never imagined his parents would be leaving this soon. "Wait," he said when he had recovered. "Today is Monday, right? Friday's only four days away—"

His parents looked at him with sympathy. "It's rough, I know," said Dad.

"Hey!" Erik said. "I can't go—Patrick and I have almost finished building the tree fort. We're going to sleep out the night after we go—" He stopped suddenly, remembering something. Something huge. Something that made leaving on Friday impossible.

"No!" he shouted. "I *can't* go on Friday! I'm going hunting with Patrick this weekend, remember?"

A pained expression passed over his dad's face. "I know how much you've been looking forward to that, Erik. I'm proud of how well you did in that course you took, and Patrick's dad tells me you're getting to be a pretty good shot. I'm really sorry, buddy. But there's always next year."

"Next year!" Erik exploded with frustration. "Dad, I've been waiting practically my whole life for this. Mr. Holt says there are grouse all over the place and he knows where there's a bunch of pheasants, too. *This* is the year! Not next year. *Now.*"

His parents shrugged helplessly. Erik knew there was nothing more they could say. For a while longer, he asked questions and his parents did their best to give cheery answers. But it was clear to him that they didn't know for certain what the future had in store for them, or for him, and that there was nothing he could do to change what was going to happen.

Finally, his mother said tiredly, "It's late, Erik, and you have school in the morning." It was a sign of how upset she was that she didn't even ask if he had homework. Not that it mattered now, Erik thought.

Upstairs, he lay on his bed, hating the Army and trying to plan how he might manage to run away from home before his parents could put him on a plane to North Dakota.

Like Patrick's pet gerbil Atlas when he got running on his wheel, Erik's brain kept circling round and round, going nowhere. He could hardly get his mind around the idea that he was going to have to live in North Dakota. What did seem real—horribly real—was that he wasn't going to be able to go hunting on Saturday. He'd been dreaming of it for as long as he could remember. He'd had to work hard to convince his mother to allow it.

When he'd first brought up the subject, his dad had shrugged and said it was okay with him, even though he didn't have any interest in hunting birds himself. But his mother had said, "Absolutely not. You're too young to handle a gun. And why do you want to shoot some poor wild creature that's never done you any harm? It's not as if you're starving, after all."

Well, no, he wasn't starving. But that wasn't the point. Erik had to think hard about how to explain it so she would understand.

"Sometimes," he began, "I wish it was still pioneer times. Kids really got to *do* things back then."

His mother looked puzzled. "Like what?"

"*Real* stuff. Important stuff. Stuff they needed to do to *survive*."

His mother nodded slowly.

He went on. "When Patrick and I camp out, we pretend we're living back in the old days. And when we're hammering and sawing on the tree fort, we pretend we're building it for shelter and we've got to hurry because winter's coming soon. We talk about how we're going to go hunting because, obviously, pioneers can't go to the grocery store to get meat. We're trying to learn all about the woods, and about the animals. Like back in the old days, when people and animals were part of the same world, you know?"

He had stopped then, feeling frustrated. He had a perfectly clear idea in his head, which made total sense to *him*, but when he tried to talk about it, it sounded dumb.

Maybe he had explained it better than he thought because, to his surprise, his mom had said she'd think about it.

And that was how he had ended up taking the hunter safety course with Patrick. There, they had learned everything they might ever need to know about handling a shotgun: how to load and unload it, how to clean it, walk with it, even how to climb over a fence with it. They learned never to assume a gun was empty, never to point a gun anywhere near another person, and never to shoot unless they could see clearly and were two hundred percent sure what they were aiming at.

Patrick's dad also began taking them to his sportsmen's club to shoot saucer-shaped targets called clay pigeons. The clay "birds" were launched from all different directions, and Erik and Patrick learned to stay alert and ready. Mr. Holt said it was good training for the field, since one never knew when a real bird might go up, or what it might do.

With each trip to the range, they'd become better and better shots. When he began to hit many more targets than he missed, Erik felt great. It was about the most fun he'd ever had. Actual hunting was going to be even more fun—and now he was going to miss out. He'd come so close. It was unbelievably unfair.

Snatches of his parents' conversation drifted up the stairs, and Erik's bitter thoughts were interrupted when he heard his name.

"I can't help worrying about Erik, going out there," his mother said. "You know how my father is. Ever since—" Her voice grew muffled as she walked from the living room into the kitchen, and Erik strained to hear. "—and I got out of there as soon as I could, and never looked back. I just wish—" Her voice grew low again and he missed what came next.

"It's been a long time," his father replied. "Maybe things have changed."

His mother murmured something Erik didn't catch. Then he heard, "—nothing I did helped. Nothing I did seemed to matter at all. Looking back, I guess joining the Army Reserves was a way of trying to get his attention." She gave a rueful laugh. "It didn't work, but at least—" Again, her voice faded out.

The next thing Erik heard was his dad saying, "Well, I'm hoping Erik might feel differently about it. There's nothing he likes more than being outdoors . . ."

His mom said, "And goodness knows there's a lot of outdoors in North Dakota."

After that, they started talking about what Erik would need while he was away, what he should pack and what they would ship. Then they discussed closing up the house and making plans for Crenshaw, and Erik stopped listening. He stared at the wall, puzzling over the things he'd overheard his mother say, and wondering about the things she'd said that he *hadn't* been able to hear.

His eyes came to rest on a sketch that hung over his dresser. His mom was attending an adult drawing class, and when he had said how much he liked one of her first pictures, she had framed it for him. In it, she had sketched in pencil a flock of Canada geese in flight. The simple lines captured everything Erik loved about seeing the V-shaped formations of geese in the sky: their freedom, their grace, and the way they flew together, taking turns as the leader.

Around the geese, in careful, flowing calligraphy, his mother had written: *Do the geese have dreams? Do they make plans as they fly? Do you? How will you live your own wild life?*

Erik hadn't really thought about the words before, but he contemplated them now. Did he have plans for his life? It seemed a cruel question. He had *planned* on finishing the tree fort and going hunting with Patrick. He'd *planned* on his life staying the way it was, before he'd walked in the door and learned he was being exiled to North Nowhere.

What good did it do a kid to make plans? Kids' lives didn't belong to them. Grownups made all the decisions, and kids just had to do what they were told.

3

Four days later Erik was on a plane to Chicago. It was only the first leg of the daylong journey he'd been dreading. When he'd told Patrick and Mr. Holt that he couldn't go hunting with them because he was going to North Dakota, Mr. Holt had tried to cheer him up.

"You lucky son of a gun!" he'd said. "I've always wanted to go out there! The pheasant hunting is fantastic! It's a bird hunter's paradise."

When Erik and Patrick had pointed out that Erik didn't own a gun himself, or a dog, either, for that matter, Mr. Holt had shaken his head with sympathy. "That's a darn shame, Erik, and I'm really sorry you won't be coming with us Saturday. But we'll go next year, you can count on it."

Which didn't make Erik feel the least bit better.

Mr. Holt gave Erik some of his hunting magazines with articles that featured North Dakota. Now, on the plane, Erik pulled them out of his backpack and tried to read, but he couldn't concentrate on the words. When the batteries in his computer game died, he fidgeted. Tapping his foot and drumming his fingers on the tray table, he watched the people around him and wondered how they could stand sitting still for so long. Weren't their legs twitchy? Didn't they want to jump up and move around, the way he did?

He took the items from the seat pocket in front of him and examined the barf bag. The woman beside him gave him a worried smile and asked if he'd like her to get up so he could visit the bathroom. Embarrassed, he said no, returned the bag to the pouch, and tried to keep his body still.

More embarrassing was the fact that he had been escorted on and would be escorted off the plane by a flight attendant, as if he were a little kid. Even worse than that, he had to wear a badge with "UM" on it, which stood for "Unaccompanied Minor." He tried to entertain himself by thinking up other things the letters could represent, like "Ugly Moron," "Upchucking Midget," "Unbalanced Madman," and "Unusual

20

Mammal." This amused him enough so that he chuckled to himself, causing the woman beside him to give him another worried glance. He stared down at his lap, willing the flight to be over.

After Chicago, he flew to Fargo, North Dakota, and from there to Minot, in a plane so small he felt like he was on an amusement park ride. He spent the whole trip looking out the window at the ground below, trying to make sense of what he was seeing. Then he realized that he was actually trying to make sense of what he *wasn't* seeing. Where *was* everything? Maybe, he thought, they were too high in the air for normal things like roads and houses and stores to be visible. But, no, that wasn't it, because every once in a while he did see a building or a road. They sure looked to be few and far between.

When the plane was about to land, Erik was astonished to see five jackrabbits hop off the runway. While he thought that was pretty funny and he liked seeing them, he couldn't help wondering if he'd come to a place with more rabbits than people.

Minot, he'd learned from the airport loudspeaker, rhymed with "why not." As he got off the plane and walked across the windy tarmac and into the airport, he could think of a lot of reasons why not.

At the end of the long hall leading from the airport gate, a tall man wearing jeans and a John Deere cap stood waiting beside a small, thin woman who reminded Erik of a nervous little bird. Even from such a distance, the intense blue of the man's eyes was striking.

Erik drew closer, and the woman's face broke into an anxious smile. He could read her lips as she said, "That's him." The man's face showed no expression. Erik knew these people must be his grandparents, but he didn't feel related to them at all. His mother had told him to greet them with a hug, but instead he hugged his backpack to his chest as he approached.

"Erik Anders Carlson, is that you?" the woman asked.

All at once Erik felt panicky and thought about shaking his head and walking past. But then what?

He nodded.

"Thank the Lord. I was worried you wouldn't make it, what with all those stops you had along the way. Why, I could barely make head or tail of that itinerary your momma sent."

She said the word *itinerary* carefully, Erik noticed, as if perhaps she were saying it out loud for the first time.

"Well, now, say hello to your grandfather."

"Hi—" Erik hesitated, embarrassed. His birthday cards were always signed "Oma and Big Darrell." While he could imagine addressing this somber man as "Sir," he couldn't bring himself to say "Big Darrell" to the man's face.

But his grandmother was urging, "Go ahead. Call him Big Darrell. Everybody does."

"Hello, B-Big Darrell," Erik said.

Big Darrell cleared his throat. "Erik," he said, in a voice filled with gravel.

"How come people call you that?" Erik asked him.

But Big Darrell had already turned away and was heading for the baggage claim area. Erik wished he could call the question back.

It was Oma who answered, as she and Erik followed Big Darrell through the light crowd of people. "It's on account of at the school he went to, there were two Darrells," she explained. "Can you imagine, in a one-room school with twelve children on a good attendance day, *two* Darrells? Anyway, tall like he is, he was the big one."

"Oh."

They waited in silence for Erik's suitcases to come around on the carousel, and then he followed his grandparents out of the terminal. They sat in the front seat of a beat-up-looking red pickup truck, with Erik in the middle. His grandmother patted his hand and told him to call her Oma. "That's how our people do. It stands for Old Ma," she said. Then she gave a dry little laugh and added, "And I expect I'm old enough."

She pointed her thumb and said, "He'd be Opa, for Old Pa, if he wasn't Big Darrell."

Erik glanced out the corner of his eye at Big Darrell, who started the engine looking straight ahead, his face set. Erik wondered what he had done to make Big Darrell mad. He'd just arrived; how could he have done anything wrong?

As they drove through Minot, he was relieved to see a lot of the same fast-food places he was accustomed to seeing at home, as well as a mall, and a theater showing eight different movies. But when they left the city behind, driving farther and farther west, the world out the window looked more and more unfamiliar. There was so much empty space, so much sky, so much *nothing*. He could see really, *really* far . . . , but there wasn't anything *to* see as they drove along what had to be the longest, straightest, flattest road in the country. Nothing except for mile after mile of flat, brown prairie, and corn and sunflower fields so big they seemed to never end.

Every once in a while, there was a grain silo or a broken-down, old white church with a tall steeple, or things that looked to Erik like big metal dinosaurs bending over to drink, leaning back to swallow, and bending over to drink again. Oma explained that they were rigs to pump oil out of the ground. Fires burned beside some of them, sending flames shooting into the open air. Oma said they were new rigs that were burning off excess methane gas. The fires looked eerie, sending their heat up into the sky.

North Dakota appeared every bit as foreign and desertlike to Erik as pictures of Iraq and Afghanistan he'd seen on TV. After they'd been driving for three and a half hours, he couldn't help wondering if they were going to the very end of the world. It had been the end for lots of people, Erik could see that. There seemed to be more abandoned houses slowly sinking into the prairie than there were ones that were inhabited.

Squished between Big Darrell and Oma on the truck's seat, he felt oddly tired and wired at the same time. Even if he had felt relaxed enough to doze off, he was sure the rattle and whistle of the truck's windows would have woken him. The wind seemed to him like some sort of crazed creature that was trying to tear its way inside the cab. Dust and—he could hardly believe it—actual *tumbleweeds* raced across the highway, with nothing to stop them in all that wide openness.

Oma knitted and Big Darrell drove, both of them seeming content to pass the ride without talking. Erik wasn't used to this, and it made him uncomfortable. In a momentary lull in the shriek of the wind he blurted, "Where are all the *people*?"

Neither of his grandparents spoke for a minute. Then Oma said, "Busy. Doing the things people do . . ." Her voice trailed off vaguely, and she gave a small shrug.

"No," Erik said, "I mean, how come there *aren't* any people? Or hardly any houses or any stores or any *anything*?"

Oma blinked. "Why, I expect it looks different here than it does in New York," she said. "But there are people. You'll see."

A while later Erik asked, "How much longer until we get there?"

"Another hour or so," said Oma.

He tried not to groan. The day seemed endless.

He'd never sat still for so long in his entire life. After what seemed much more than an hour, Big Darrell turned off the highway by a sign whose paint had peeled so badly Erik had to squint hard to make out what it said. FORTUNA, N.D.—YOU'LL ♥ IT. Painted around the words were four pictures: a motor home, a cow, a tractor, and a pheasant.

The sight of the pheasant cheered Erik for a couple of seconds, until he remembered that tomorrow he was supposed to be home, hunting actual pheasants with Patrick.

As Big Darrell drove slowly down a street that was lined with boarded-up dingy storefronts, Erik looked around with a sinking heart. Everything was dusty, and rusty, and old. He thought that a buzzard would be a far more appropriate symbol for the place than a pheasant. He knew right then and there that he wasn't going to ♥ Fortuna, not one bit.

There were clues, such as the presence of cars and tractors, a string of limp telephone wires lining the street, and a satellite dish on a rooftop, that told him he hadn't actually gone back in time to the old Wild West.

But he sure as heck knew a ghost town when he saw one.

4

Big Darrell pulled into a dumpy-looking gas station Erik would have guessed was out of business, and got out to work the pump.

"Fortuna's only got a few streets," Oma explained while she and Erik waited. "So it's real simple to find your way around."

Erik almost said what he was thinking: *As if anybody could possibly get lost in such a dinky place.*

"All the businesses are closed now," Oma went on, "except for this gas station and the tavern." She pointed to a dilapidated building with a neon beer advertisement in the window. "We have to go clear to Crosby for groceries. There's only eleven houses here that still have folks living in 'em."

They had passed a few houses, all of which had a

sad, run-down look. Erik wasn't convinced that people actually lived in any of them. There was a lot of old stuff scattered about the yards, too: rusty car bodies and farm machinery, a bike, a washing machine, a deflated plastic swimming pool. It was hard to figure why people would keep junk like that around. It wasn't as if there was nowhere else to put it. There was nothing but empty space out here. He felt his spirits dip even lower.

"Mom said you sold the farm. Where's your house?" he asked, hoping it wasn't one of the ones he'd already seen.

"Oh, we don't live here in town," said Oma. "We still live out at the farm, where your momma grew up. We just sold the land. Jim Lund bought it. Big Darrell still works with Jim every day. You can't imagine Big Darrell not farming, can you?"

Erik didn't know what to say to that, so he didn't answer. Instead, he said, "Where *is* the farm?"

"I guess you don't remember much from your visit, it was such a long time ago," Oma answered. "It's out a ways."

"Out a ways" turned out to be miles down a part-dirt and part-gravel road off the main highway. It was beginning to get dark. As they jounced along over the ruts, three deer appeared, seemingly out of nowhere, running across a field to the right of the truck. Erik knew immediately that they were mule deer, not white-tails like they had in New York. These were the first mulies he'd ever seen! He couldn't wait to tell Patrick about them.

Oma noticed him looking at them and patted his knee. "We have to be real careful driving at night around here. The deer start moving at dusk. I can't think of a soul who hasn't had a run-in with one, or at least a close call. Can you, Big Darrell?"

Big Darrell might have shaken his head no, but it was hard to tell. A little farther along, Erik was amazed to see a group of about twenty pheasants standing on the edge of the ditch by the side of the road. He couldn't help reaching across his grandfather to point, crying out, "Look! Over there! Pheasants! A bunch of 'em!"

"Oh, heavens, there's pheasants all over the place this year," Oma declared. "Last year we had a mild winter, so they did real well. Jim Lund was just saying yesterday you can hardly swing a dead cat without hitting one."

Erik twisted around in his seat so he could watch the birds until they were out of sight. "What are they all doing in the road?" he wondered aloud.

"They're out in the crops all day, eating," Big Darrell said. "Heading back to cover for the night."

It seemed to Erik as if his grandfather had spoken in spite of himself, almost as if the words had forced themselves from between his lips. Still, these were more words than he had uttered all afternoon. Encouraged, Erik asked, "Can we hunt them?"

Both Big Darrell and Oma stiffened in their seats, and a charged silence filled the truck cab. Finally, Oma said quietly, "Big Darrell's too busy for hunting these days."

Erik suddenly felt desperate to escape the tense, strained atmosphere in the small enclosure of the truck's cab. His brief feeling of happiness at seeing the deer and pheasants drained away. Oma broke the silence finally, saying in an overly cheery voice, "Well, here we are!"

On the right, a gravel driveway led to a two-story wooden farmhouse. Erik searched his memory, but he had no feeling of recognition for the place. He could tell the house had once been painted white, and the two shutters that were left had once been red. The roof sagged, and the whole thing sort of slumped to the left, as if it had grown weary of fighting the wind. Everything looked old and poor and ready to give up.

There was a big barn, too, and some smaller buildings, and a lot of large farm machinery, like tractors and combines and others he didn't know the names of. As Big Darrell pulled up beside a pile of neatly stacked firewood, Erik pointed to a narrow little building with the shape of a crescent moon cut into the door. "Is that—um . . . is that what I think it is?" he asked.

"Why, that's the outhouse, Erik," Oma answered.

His face must have shown his dismay, because Oma laughed and added, "There's a bathroom inside. But the outhouse comes in handy during mud season when the men are out here working and their boots get all dirty."

Erik thought, *If my feet get muddy, I'm taking off my shoes and going inside.*

Oma got out of the truck with a low groan. "Come on in," she said, "but mind the porch steps. One's broken. Stay to the right when you go up."

Big Darrell got Erik's suitcases from the truck bed and walked toward the house. Erik's legs were numb from the long ride, and he had to force himself to move. When he slid from the truck seat to the ground, a fierce blast of wind snatched at him, nearly knocking him over. Pushing his hair out of his eyes, he looked around in the gathering darkness.

There wasn't another house as far as he could see. There were fields, and a straight line of trees to one side of the house, which he figured had been planted in a vain effort to try to break the wind. The trees led to a low area where some scrubby-looking bushes grew. There might have been a pond down there, but it was too dark now to tell.

The first stars were appearing, and as he looked up at them he felt dizzy, lost in all the endless space stretching out in every direction. He closed his eyes as he was buffeted by another blast of wind. The wind here was different from at home. Here, it seemed to him to have a will of its own, as if it were determined to clear the land of anything too weak to withstand its relentless pressure. He bent into it and climbed onto the porch, being careful to put his weight on the only two steps that looked solid, and went into the house.

Oma stood at the bottom of the stairs that led up to the second floor. "I'll show you your room. You go first. These old legs of mine are awful slow."

Wordlessly, Big Darrell handed over one of the suitcases and Erik started up the stairs with it. Oma came next, and Big Darrell followed with the other suitcase. Erik hesitated at the top, then reached for the knob on the first door he came to. He was about to turn it when Oma drew a sharp breath.

"*No,*" Big Darrell said. The single word, spoken forcefully in his deep, hoarse voice, hung in the air.

Erik pulled back his hand in surprise and turned around. Big Darrell's face was hidden in the shadows, but Oma's eyes were wide with alarm. Quickly, she recovered herself and gave a small, nervous laugh. "Not that one, Erik. The next one, farther down on the right."

Slowly, Erik turned to the door across the hall, half expecting another outburst. But Oma opened it and flicked a light switch. Sounding slightly out of breath, she said, "Here you are."

Without speaking, Big Darrell set the suitcase on the floor in the hallway and went back down the stairs. Oma and Erik stood looking around the room. "Just like your momma left it," Oma said, "except we've ended up storing a few things in here, you know how that goes . . ."

A few things? Erik thought incredulously. There was a single bed, covered neatly in a faded blue-flowered spread, and a dresser with a mirror attached. But the floor was piled with random *stuff*—a fake Christmas tree in a stand, a sewing machine, cardboard boxes, and several bulging plastic bags. A narrow path snaked through it all, making it possible to walk from the door to the dresser or from the door to the bed.

Doesn't anybody around here ever throw anything out? Erik wondered.

Oma was looking around, too, with a funny expression on her face. He had the feeling she was really seeing the room for the first time in a while. "I expect we'll need to move some of this to the attic," she said uncertainly. "Give you a little more space."

When Erik didn't say anything, Oma said, "You just go ahead and make yourself at home, now, while I get some supper started."

Erik had a sudden hopeful thought. "The school," he said. "Is it closed, too, like all the stores in town?"

"Oh, there's no school in Fortuna," she replied.

Wow, he thought. *I have actually come to a place so far out in the middle of nowhere that there isn't even a school!* This news would have been thrilling if he could have thought of one thing to do here *besides* going to school.

Oma said, "You'll be going to the Crosby Middle School. I let them know you were coming, and the bus will be stopping for you out by the highway."

Erik didn't know whether to feel disappointed or relieved. He'd been trying hard not to think about the prospect of starting school at a new place where he didn't know anybody. But what was he going to do with himself for the next two days before school began on Monday?

When Oma left, Erik sat on the bed looking around the tiny room. This must be what it felt like to be in a jail cell in Siberia, except his cell had the added attraction of being filled with junk.

5

Erik didn't unpack. That would be like admitting he was going to be staying for a while, and part of his mind simply refused to accept that. With nothing else to do, he poked around the room that had once belonged to his mother. Some photos and papers were stuck in the frame around the mirror over the dresser, and he examined them. One picture showed his mom when she was little, standing beside a brown and white calf with a blue ribbon around its neck. She was grinning proudly at the camera. There were several other blue and red ribbons from the Fortuna 4-H, a medal from a school track meet, and a program from a school play in which her part was listed as "Blue Fairy."

There were a couple of shots of her and an older boy, one where they were smiling and sitting on top of hay bales piled in the bed of a pickup truck, another of them dressed for trick-or-treat. Erik looked closely at the series of school pictures that showed his mother growing from a cute, toothless kid into a cute teenager. In the early pictures, when she was elementary-school and middle-school age, she looked out at the camera with a wide, easy, confident, and, Erik thought, somewhat mischievous smile.

But then, in what he figured were her high school pictures, something changed. The crinkly-eyed, mischievous smile was gone, replaced by a flat, solemn expression. He'd seen kids put on that expression when they wanted to appear cool. Maybe that was what she'd been trying to do, but Erik thought it made her look sad.

Oma called to him to say supper was almost ready. He felt uncomfortable entering the living room where Big Darrell was sitting on a worn-looking chair watching the news, though he was really glad to see the television. *Where there's TV, there's hope,* he told himself.

From the kitchen, Oma said, "Goodness, it's seven-thirty! We don't usually eat anywhere near this late.

Erik, I told your momma you'd call her when we got in. Better do it now, so she won't worry. It's two hours later there."

Erik had forgotten about the time difference. No wonder the day had seemed so long. As he picked up the phone, Big Darrell spoke. "That's long-distance to New York."

Well, duh, thought Erik. *I'm the one who just traveled all the way across the country.* He turned to look at Big Darrell, to see if maybe he was kidding around. Big Darrell had removed the cap he'd been wearing on the drive from the airport, and Erik was momentarily startled by the whiteness of his grandfather's forehead compared to the rest of his tanned and ruddy complexion. His face didn't show a trace of humor.

Oma appeared at the doorway between the kitchen and the living room. "Oh, he won't talk long. Now, will you, Erik?" she asked, sounding flustered.

So that's what's bugging him, Erik realized. *Big Darrell's worried that I'll run up his telephone bill, the cheapskate.* "I can use my cell phone," he said, reaching into his pocket. But as soon as the connection was made, a message came up saying, "Call Was Lost!"

He tried several times without success. Oma, who had been watching, said, "I don't know much about those things, but most folks around here use a certain company, I forget the name. What is it, Big Darrell, do you recall?"

Big Darrell shook his head.

"Well, the name doesn't matter. But it's likely a different—" She paused, her brow furrowed, as she tried to come up with the right word.

"Network?" Erik suggested.

She brightened and smiled at him. "That's right. It's different here."

It's different, all right, Erik thought.

"I could just e-mail her," he said. "She's online a lot."

"Oh, goodness," said Oma. "You need a computer for that, don't you?"

Erik nodded, his heart sinking.

"We don't have one of those. I don't really understand what on earth people are doing, staring at those things all day."

Erik couldn't believe it. He was trapped in a house without a cell phone or a computer. It was like a nightmare.

Oma handed him an old-fashioned telephone with a coiled cord. "Here. You go ahead and call your momma. I expect she'd rather hear your voice, any-how."

When his mother asked, he told her that the plane trip had been torture. She asked a few more cheerful questions, but he was having no part of being cheered up. He wanted to tell her how awful everything was, how he couldn't believe she had sent him to this creepy house with her scary, mean old father who never talked, a place that had no school, where his cell phone didn't work, where there were no other kids, no com-puter, no *nothing* except junk and, oh, right, don't for-get, an outhouse. He couldn't say what he wanted to say, not with Oma fussing about the kitchen and the Great Stone Face sitting in the living room listening.

"I've got to go, Mom. Oma's putting dinner on the table."

"All right, sweetie," said his mom. "I'm glad you're there safe and sound. Are you sure you're okay? You sound a little funny."

"Oh, everything's just great," he said.

His mother must have heard the sarcasm in his voice, and sighed. "We'll call you every chance we get, but it's going to be tricky, with the time difference. They tell us we'll be able to e-mail you."

"That would work," Erik whispered into the phone. "*If* there was a computer here. Which there isn't."

"Yes, I know. But there must be computers at the public library in Crosby," his mother said. "And I'm sure they'll have them at school."

Erik didn't answer.

"We can write letters, too," said his mom. "It'll be like pioneer days. You should like that."

Again, Erik didn't answer. Into the silence his mother said, "You *will* write, won't you?"

"I guess."

"Meanwhile, you try to make the best of things, okay? And help Oma."

"Um-hmm," Erik said without enthusiasm.

"Try to have a positive outlook."

"Right."

"Bye, sweetie. I love you. I'm going to put your dad on."

Erik waited, knowing that he'd undoubtedly hurt her feelings by not saying he loved her back. But he didn't feel like saying it right then.

"Erik?"

"Hi, Dad."

"How's it going?"

"Terrific."

His father chose to take his words at face value. "Well, that's great. I didn't think it would be as bad as you thought it would be."

Actually, it's worse, Erik wanted to say.

"It's hard to believe we're going halfway around the world tomorrow. We'll stay in the best touch we can, okay, buddy?"

"Okay."

"We'll see each other before we know it."

"Yeah."

"Hang in there, son. I love you."

"Yup. Okay. Bye, Dad."

Erik hung up and sat at the table, where Oma and Big Darrell were waiting to serve supper. The meal was almost as quiet as the ride from Minot, only now they had a few things to say, like "Pass the applesauce, please," and "Would you like some more peas?" and "No, thanks."

After dinner Big Darrell went upstairs and Oma explained that he kept "farmer's hours," going to bed and getting up very early. When Erik turned on the TV and discovered that it only got three channels and the picture was fuzzy, he said he was tired, too, and went to his room.

He lay in the bed that used to be his mother's and

stared at the ceiling, wondering how he was going to survive six months—maybe longer!—in this place. He tossed fitfully, mad at himself for not being able to fall asleep when all he wanted was for the longest and worst day of his life to come to an end.

6

In the morning, Erik waited until he heard Big Darrell drive off before he came downstairs.

"It's sugar beet harvest, Erik," Oma explained as she fried him some bacon and eggs. "Big Darrell's helping out a cousin of Jim's down near Williston, so he'll be out until after dark."

When he'd finished his breakfast, Oma told him a friend was picking her up to work on a fall festival they were organizing at the church. She asked him if he wanted to go, but he said no.

"Well," she said vaguely, "I expect you'll be just fine on your own. There are leftovers from last night for lunch."

She carefully wrote the phone number of the church

on a tablet and set it on the counter. Then her friend's car pulled up outside and she left.

It appeared he wasn't going to have to worry about his grandparents smothering him with attention, which was just fine with him.

Idly, he turned on the TV, flipped through the three channels checking out the grainy pictures, and turned it off. Then he wandered around the living room, but there wasn't much to see except for Oma's coupon organizer and her knitting patterns, and some farm journals of Big Darrell's. He was surprised to see all of his own school pictures, framed and carefully arranged in order, beginning with his kindergarten shot and ending with last year's sixth-grade picture, which was a disaster. His mother had taken him to the barber the day before, where he'd gotten scalped. In the photo, he looked like a pinhead with enormous ears.

It was weird to think that these strangers out in North Dakota had his photos prominently displayed in the living room. With a sigh, he faced the serious question of what he was going to do to keep from going crazy. No answers came to mind, so he started up to his room. Not that there was anything to do there, either, except rearrange the junk in new and different piles.

At the top of the stairs, he recalled the night before when he'd been about to go into the room across the hall from his, the one on the left. His grandfather had cried out, "No!" *Sheesh. What was the big deal, anyway?*

He thought of movies he'd seen in which there was a house with a forbidden room, which turned out to hold a terrible secret or else was once the scene of a gruesome murder. He laughed out loud. How likely was it that anything half that interesting lay behind a door in his grandparents' house in the middle of nowhere? He should be so lucky.

Even so, he wanted to open that door. He pretty much *had* to open that door.

He paused, his hand on the knob, feeling he was doing something wrong. *That's stupid,* he told himself. It wasn't as if he'd been told to stay out. The more he thought about it, the more he wondered if his grandparents had actually reacted as strongly as he'd thought. Probably the room was really messy and Oma was embarrassed at the way it looked, the way his mother always acted when company showed up unexpectedly—though it was kind of hard to imagine that a room could be more disorderly than the one he was staying in.

He turned the knob and stepped inside. To his surprise, the room wasn't at all messy, but perfectly neat and tidy. *Oddly neat and tidy,* he thought, especially compared to the rest of the house. He looked around, at the framed photograph on the dresser of a proud, smiling young soldier in uniform, at the American flag on the wall, at the dog tags and the gold heart-shaped medal hanging from a purple ribbon, and all at once he understood.

This was his uncle's room, the uncle he'd never met, his mother's brother, Dan, who had died in Vietnam when his mother was fourteen. Erik had almost forgotten about Dan. His mother never talked about him. She said it made her too sad. All Erik really knew about Dan was that his mom had loved him and he was dead.

It felt wrong to be here. Suddenly unable to breathe, he left the room that was Dan's shrine and shut the door behind him.

7

Desperate to get out of the house, Erik put on his jacket and walked onto the porch. It was a nice day, he realized. The sun shone and the persistent wind of the night before had lowered to a whisper. He was amazed again by the prairie spreading so far in all directions, with no house in sight and no signs of other people. The sky looked so big. Gazing up, he thought of his parents, who were probably in an airplane at that very moment. It hardly seemed real. He felt very small all of a sudden, and even lonelier and farther from home.

Wandering aimlessly around the yard, he kicked up gravel in the driveway and checked out the combines and tractors. The tires on some of those monsters were higher than the top of his head! He tried to imagine what it would be like to drive one.

Then his eyes fell on the outhouse. He'd never been in an outhouse before. Would it be really stinky? He opened the door cautiously, prepared to shut it fast, but to his relief it didn't smell bad at all. Maybe because it wasn't used much.

The open door let in enough light to see, and he observed with a grin that this was a two-hole model. He'd heard of such things but could never quite get his mind around the idea. He tried to picture sitting side by side out here with someone else, and doing—*what?* Having a friendly conversation? Looking straight ahead and pretending the other person wasn't there?

He shook his head. As he'd explained to his mother, he often wished he lived back in the days of the pioneers, but in this particular regard, he was grateful for modern conveniences. He read the sign posted on the wall above some stacked rolls of toilet paper, which said, "The job ain't finished 'til the paperwork is done," and cracked up. It was his first laugh since arriving in North Dakota, and it felt good.

There was a pile of ratty old *Life* magazines on the seat bench, and that was about it. He was ready to leave when he heard a noise outside. He froze, listening.

It sounded to Erik like someone *panting*, as if he'd been running hard. But who would have run all the way out here? Then he heard just the slightest whimper. Was it a whimper of pain or fear, or something else? He was spooked by the strange sound, but he couldn't very well hide in the outhouse and hope whoever it was went away.

Cautiously, he pushed the door open wider and peered out. From the corner of his eye, he saw something move into the barn. He caught only a quick glimpse of a shape, enough to know it wasn't a person but an animal, although what kind he hadn't been able to tell. He wasn't quite sure of the size, either.

He walked slowly to the big barn door, which slid from side to side on a metal track and was now halfway open. Slipping inside, he waited for his eyes to grow accustomed to the dim light. He was vaguely aware of the pleasant smells of earth, grain, motor oil, and hay; aware, too, of his racing heart, as he imagined some crazed, slathering beast springing at him from the gloom. Did they have wolves out here? He didn't know. He hoped not.

Soon he could pick out the forms of different objects: a workbench with tools, some shovels and rakes leaning against the wall, scraps of lumber, bales of hay, sacks of what he figured was fertilizer, and an old, beat-up car. Then, in the corner by the stacks of hay bales, he saw movement.

Listening hard, he heard it again: panting, followed by a whimper, and another.

He looked in vain for a light switch. Sliding the barn door all the way open to let in some daylight, he began walking very slowly toward the sound. Knowing that a cornered animal can be dangerous, he approached the hay bales from the side, to leave the creature an escape route. If it didn't want him any closer, it could choose to run for the door rather than attack. He hoped.

As he drew nearer, he could hear the animal panting harder and could see that it was shaking, but he still couldn't make out what it was. He wondered what kinds of animals lived out here that he might not know about. How big were badgers and what did they look like? What about coyotes?

Closer now, he could see that the animal was about the same size as a dog, not a big dog, but not a small one, either. Medium-sized. Its fur was mottled, and its head appeared dark, but there was something really, really odd-looking about it.

The creature whimpered in earnest then and lifted its head, and the picture became clear. It *was* a dog. And sticking out from its muzzle were about a hundred of what he immediately knew must be porcupine quills. Whitish tan in color and an inch to two inches long, they covered the dog's entire nose and bristled angrily from its mouth and from the area close to its eyes.

Erik gasped and stopped, horrified, not knowing what to do. He tried to remember what he'd read or heard about porcupine quills. He was pretty sure they had barbs on the ends that made them really difficult to remove. And that they were terribly, terribly painful.

"It's going to be okay, boy," he said softly and soothingly. "Don't worry. I'll figure something out. We'll fix you up, boy, don't worry."

Despite its obvious pain, the dog gazed up at him and—he could scarcely believe it—wagged the tip of its stubby tail back and forth several times. Then it rose unsteadily to its feet and looked at him uncertainly.

"Don't worry, boy," Erik said, trying to keep his voice low and reassuring in spite of his racing heart. "I'm not going to hurt you any more."

He'd heard stories of people pulling out porcupine quills with pliers, but thinking about how much that would hurt the dog made him feel queasy inside. The idea of calling a vet raced through his mind, but he didn't know who to call, or whether vets even made house calls, especially for a kid they didn't know. Then he remembered that Oma had left the church phone number inside on the counter.

"I'm going to go call for help now, okay, boy? Don't worry. I'm not deserting you. I'll be right back, I promise. Okay? Just hang on, okay?"

The dog gave a low whine, and Erik tore himself away. Afraid the dog might run off while he was gone, he closed the barn door and ran to the house.

He dialed the number Oma had left, and was momentarily taken aback when a strange woman answered, saying, "Red Butte Lutheran Church."

"Is Oma—I mean, is—" Erik panicked for a moment, unable for the life of him to think of Oma's real name. "I'm looking for my grandmother, she's—"

"This'll be Erik, then?" the woman said.

"Yes! Yes, that's me. Is Oma there?"

"You betcha she is, young man," the woman said kindly. "And she's so happy you've come to visit. Why, she was just telling me how big you are, and how——"

"Excuse me," Erik said desperately, "I'm sorry to interrupt, but this is kind of—an emergency."

"Oh, my! Goodness! Just a minute. I'll get her." The phone clattered as she put it down, and Erik heard her call, "Grace! Grace, you'd better put down that crepe paper and come to the phone, quick, now!"

After a moment, Oma picked up the phone and said breathlessly, "Erik, is that you? What's happened? Are you all right?"

"I'm fine," he said quickly. "It's just that I—I found a dog. It's out in the barn, and its whole face is full of porcupine quills, and I didn't know what to do, and I wondered if you could call a vet or something."

"Oh, dear," said Oma. "The poor thing. Let me think . . . I'll call our friend Bob Thompson and ask him if he'll come out to the house. He's a veterinarian."

Erik felt suddenly weak with relief.

"Erik, listen to me," Oma went on. "In the meantime, don't you go near that dog, you hear? If it's in pain, you don't know what it might do."

"Okay," he said. "I won't." He didn't mention that

he'd already gone near the dog, and it had done nothing more than wag its tail. Erik wasn't sure why, but
he felt certain the dog wouldn't bite him. There was
no need to say this to Oma, however.

"You stay put, now, until I get home."

"I will. And, Oma? Please *hurry*."

8

Erik couldn't stay put, despite his promise to Oma. He went back out to the barn, where the dog remained curled up by the hay bales. Erik approached slowly, speaking softly. The dog's brown eyes found his and didn't waver as he walked up and knelt down. Now that he was a little more calm, Erik noticed that the dog wasn't wearing a collar. Did that mean it was a stray? Its ribs showed clearly, and Erik wondered how many days it had been suffering, hungry, yet unable to eat because of the quills.

With great care, he reached out and gently stroked the dog's side. "The vet is on his way, boy," he said. "Hang on."

It seemed as if hours passed before Erik heard a car pull into the driveway. He got up and watched from the barn door as Oma's friend dropped her off. Just seconds later the vet arrived, and Erik called them both over to the barn. Oma introduced him to "Dr. Bob," and they all went inside to where the dog lay.

Dr. Bob examined it quickly. "It's bad, but I've seen worse," he said cheerfully. "Erik, I'll need you to hold her still while I pull out the quills."

"Me?" Erik asked with surprise. He hadn't anticipated being asked to help.

"Oh, Doc, I don't know," Oma said uncertainly. "Is that safe? I don't recognize this dog. I don't think it belongs to anybody I know. I can't have anything happening to Erik. He's my daughter Darlene's boy, you know."

"Don't worry, Grace. She seems very good-natured," Dr. Bob answered, echoing the very thing that Erik had sensed about the dog. And he had called the dog a *she*.

"Sorry, girl," Erik murmured. "I didn't realize."

"Some dogs react to pain and fear with aggression," Dr. Bob went on, "but I think she's going to be okay." Looking at Oma, he added, "If I'm wrong, I'll take her back to my office and anesthetize her. But, in my opinion, it probably won't be necessary. Compared to some dogs I've seen, the porky let her off easy."

"Well, Doc, you know best," said Oma. "But I'm going back to the house. I can't bear to watch."

Dr. Bob, speaking in the same low, soothing voice Erik had tried to use before, positioned the dog and showed Erik how to hold her. "Keep talking to her," he said.

Erik did as he was told. Dr. Bob drew a pair of forceps from his bag. Gripping firmly onto the base of the first quill, he pulled, hard and fast.

The dog flinched violently and yelped. The sound wrenched Erik's heart, but he got hold of her again, gently but firmly, and kept up a steady stream of comforting words. One by one, Dr. Bob carefully and methodically pulled out the rest of the quills.

"The small ones are the hardest," he explained as he worked. "They're the ones that tend to break off. She's lucky; this must have been a pretty quick encounter. There aren't any in her tongue."

Erik shuddered at the thought.

"Sometimes," the vet continued quietly, "if the dog shakes the porcupine, the quills will get in their ears and all along the sides of their face and neck. Then, if they start to roll to relieve the pain, they end up driving the quills in farther."

Erik held on, very glad that this dog had been

smart enough not to roll. He was happy, too, to note that, after the first few quills were out, she'd begun to settle down. Never once did he fear she was going to bite him. Rather, she turned her head toward him for a moment with a look so full of trust he had the feeling that if she could talk she would have said, "I know you don't mean to hurt me. I know you're trying to help."

"Such a brave girl," he crooned. "Such a brave pup you are. Hang on now, it won't be much longer. Hang on, that's right, hang on, that's good, hang on, good girl."

Dr. Bob continued to talk to Erik as he worked. "A lot of people think porcupines are nasty animals and that they actually shoot or throw their quills. But the truth is they're gentle little guys who just want to be left alone. A person or another animal has to come in direct contact with their tail in order to get stuck."

"Those quills have barbs, right?" Erik asked.

Dr. Bob held up a quill so Erik could get a close look. There was no hook on the end, as he had imagined. The tip looked stiff, sharp and pointy.

"Another myth," Dr. Bob said matter-of-factly. "There are tiny, microscopic scales that point backwards, but no actual barbs. Thank goodness," he added. "They're the devil to get out as it is."

Finally it was over. Dr. Bob gave the dog an injection of antibiotics. Then he swabbed her face with alcohol, which she didn't like at all, followed by some antibiotic cream, which she seemed to like a lot.

Dr. Bob laughed as she licked off all the cream he had just applied. "The shot'll take care of any infection. Now, her face might be a little swollen tonight, but that's normal."

"Okay," Erik said uncertainly.

Dr. Bob said, "That's assuming you're going to take care of her until her owner shows up." He looked at Erik, eyebrows raised in a question.

"I-I'd like to," Erik said. "But, well, I guess it's up to my grandmother."

"Let's go ask her," said Dr. Bob.

They stood up and so did the dog. "Come on, girl," Erik said. He wasn't certain she'd follow them to the house, but she did.

Oma met them at the kitchen door.

"Can she come in?" Erik asked.

Oma hesitated, then nodded.

Inside, the dog sniffed around a bit, then came and stood by Erik's side. Dr. Bob said to Oma, "That went really well, and I think she's going to be fine. Erik here says he's willing to take care of her for now, if that's okay with you. Otherwise, I can take her with me."

Oma's eyes grew wide. Then, blinking nervously, she said, "Well, I don't know . . ."

"I've never seen this pup before, but I doubt it will be long until we track down her owner," Dr. Bob went on.

"I thought maybe she was a stray," said Erik.

"No, I think she must have just slipped her collar. She's a purebred German shorthaired pointer. Pheasant season just opened, and sharp-tail grouse season's been open for a while, so probably someone was hunting birds with her. Whoever it was will be looking for her, I'm sure. She's a valuable dog."

Oma considered this, a concerned expression on her face.

"Please, Oma," Erik whispered. "Can I?"

"I-It's just—it's just that . . . well, we haven't had a dog in over thirty years. When our dog Elvis died, Big Darrell said, 'No more dogs.' So I don't know . . ." Her voice drifted off again, and she looked worried.

"I'll ask him," Erik rushed to say. The words were out before he realized it. The idea of facing Big Darrell with a request was more than a little intimidating. But he couldn't let the dog leave with Dr. Bob. If she left, Erik would never see her again, he knew it.

Oma looked at him, her lips creased with worry. Then she turned to Dr. Bob, let out a long breath, and asked, "It'll most likely be just the one night, you think?"

"Sometimes people abandon dogs, and that could be what's happened here. But, as I said, I doubt someone would do that with a purebred pointer. A day or two should tell the story. She may have already been reported missing. I'll check with the police and humane society and my colleagues when I get back to the office."

"Well, then, I suppose . . ."

Before she could think it over further, Erik wrapped her small frame in a hug. "Thanks, Oma!"

Afterwards, she looked flustered, but pleased.

"Well, that's settled, then," Dr. Bob said. "If nobody's claimed her by Monday, bring her in. I'll want to check her over, anyway, to make sure she's healing the way she should. If you want, you can leave her with me then, and I'll see what I can do about finding her a home."

Oma nodded, looking relieved.

"Right now, she could use a good meal and plenty

of water. She's not emaciated, but she's pretty thin. Probably hasn't been able to eat since she tangled with that porcupine."

"Hey, Doc," said Erik. "You called her a pup. How old is she, anyway?"

"I'd say she's right around a year, give or take a month or so."

Erik reached down to give the dog a pat and murmured, "Poor puppy."

He and Oma thanked the vet, and Erik offered to pay him out of his allowance money.

Dr. Bob shook his head and smiled. "No charge. I'm glad I could help."

After they said their goodbyes, Erik knelt beside the dog. She licked his face. He laughed, and she looked at him with her left eyebrow lifted, which made her look so funny he laughed again. She answered with a singsongy little howl, then danced backward for a few steps, before coming back to lie down with her head in his lap. Erik rubbed behind her ears and felt her body relax under his touch. Then she closed her eyes in what looked like pure contentment.

Until this very moment, Erik hadn't even known he wanted a dog. But he wanted this dog so much it hurt to think of giving her up. He didn't know how it was possible to feel so connected to a creature he'd only known for a couple of hours. But he did. There was a bond between them, the boy and the dog. It had been forged in the moments when their eyes held as the quills were being removed. Erik knew she felt it, too.

She was *his*.

9

Erik glanced up to see Oma watching him with an odd expression on her face. She turned away quickly, but not before he saw the shine of tears in her eyes.

"What's the matter, Oma?" he asked. He wondered what he had done wrong now. Or if maybe she was already regretting her decision.

She shook her head, as if to clear away an unwanted thought, and said, "Nothing's wrong, dear. It's just that, for a minute there, the two of you reminded me of—well, I'm just being silly."

There was silence for a moment. Then, before Erik could say anything, she changed the subject. "Dr. Bob said to feed her, poor thing, but I don't have any dog food. What shall we give her?" Oma considered this as she set a bowl of water on the floor. Then she snapped her fingers and said, "I know!" She went to the freezer, took out a package wrapped in white paper, and held it up. "Ground venison," she said. "Best meat there is."

"That's what my friend Patrick's father says," Erik told her. "I've never had it, though."

"Oh, wait until you try it," said Oma as she put the meat in a frying pan. "Your friend's father is right. Big Darrell used to get a deer every year until—" Once again she hesitated, then measured her words. "Well, until he stopped hunting. Now Jim Lund gives us a share of his. Helps us get through the winter."

As the meat cooked, the dog's nose began to twitch eagerly. She watched intently as Oma pushed the frozen glob around with a spatula, breaking it up as it slowly browned.

When it was cooked through, Oma let it cool, then scraped it into a plastic dish and placed it on the floor. The dog walked over and sniffed the food with great interest.

"What a lady," said Oma with a laugh. "Why, Elvis would have wolfed that down in two seconds."

"Go ahead, girl," Erik urged. "It's for you."

The dog began to eat in earnest. It made Erik happy to watch her, knowing how hungry she had to be.

"Erik," said Oma quietly, "it would be best not to mention Elvis. Or to say anything to Big Darrell about giving the dog meat from the freezer . . ."

"Meat?" Erik said, pulling an innocent face. "What meat?"

Oma's laugh rang through the kitchen. It sounded nice. He wanted to ask her about Elvis, but the dog was obviously a sensitive subject, even though he'd been dead for thirty years. He didn't want to make Oma sad again.

Using an old blanket Oma gave him, Erik made a bed for the dog in the corner of the living room. She rested peacefully on it, and Erik sat beside her, stroking her, taking in every feature: the velvety softness of her ears, her warm, earthy smell, the pattern of large brown spots on her mottled coat, the rise and fall of her chest as she breathed. What really killed him was the way she looked right into his eyes. It was like she *knew* him in a way he'd never been known before.

He stayed with the dog all day, or she stayed with him. Whenever he got up, even to get a glass of milk, she followed. Erik wanted her to rest, so he got some pillows off the couch and leaned against the wall beside her bed.

Please, Dr. Bob, he willed, *do not call. Please don't let there be an owner, who will take her away.*

As the hours passed, it became impossible to think and speak of her as "the dog." Erik knew someone had probably given her a name, but he had no idea what it was and he wanted to call her something. He thought about it all afternoon, but couldn't come up with anything.

He and Oma had a quiet supper. Afterwards, she set aside a plate for Big Darrell, who still hadn't returned from harvesting beets, and switched on the news. Erik sat down beside the dog, scratched her ears, and was glad to see her close her eyes.

"That's a good girl," he murmured. "You need to sleep, poor pup, you fought with a porcupine, you were full of quills, you brave little quilly dog."

All afternoon long, he'd been whispering a similar stream of nonsense and—he might as well admit it—*baby talk*. But hearing himself now, he sat up straighter and repeated "quilly dog." He liked the sound of it. "Hey," he said, "what about Quilly?" He thought for a moment, and added, "Or maybe just Quill. What do you think about that for a name?"

The dog lifted her head and looked him square in the eye.

"*Quill,*" he repeated. "Do you like it?"

The dog lifted her left eyebrow, then lowered it.

"What do you think? You want to be Quill?"

She thumped her short tail, put her head on his lap, gave a deep, contented sigh, and closed her eyes again.

That settled *that*.

Erik was just telling Oma that he'd come up with a perfect name for the dog, when the door opened and Big Darrell walked in. His clothes and face were dusty, and when he took off his farmer's cap Erik was once again struck by the blazing blue of his eyes and the contrast between his pale forehead and the rest of his face. He hung the cap on a hook by the door and was leaning down to unlace his boots when his gaze fell on Erik and the dog. He jerked upright, as if *he'd* just been stuck by a porcupine, and stared.

After what felt to Erik like a very long time, Big Darrell asked, "What's that dog doing in here?" His deep voice sounded to Erik like a growl.

Erik stood up. Quill stirred and rose to her feet, too. With her stubby tail wagging, she approached Big Darrell. He ignored her.

Oma jumped up from her seat in front of the TV and started to say, "Darrell, it's only for—"

But Big Darrell cut her off. "Didn't I say no more dogs?"

Erik couldn't help himself. "But that was a long time ago!"

Big Darrell's face froze. He stiffened, and for a moment no one moved. He turned slowly to Erik and said deliberately, "What do you know about what happened here a long time ago?"

Erik, taken aback by the coldness in Big Darrell's gaze, stammered, "N-Nothing. I—"

"That's right. Nothing. Remember that." He turned back to Oma, who looked every bit as frightened as Erik felt. Erik could hardly bear looking at her, wringing her hands and blinking with anxiety.

"But, Darrell, I—" Oma began.

Big Darrell interrupted. "Didn't I say *no more dogs?*"

"Yes, but let me ex—"

"There's nothing to explain," Big Darrell said flatly. "The dog goes."

"It's not Oma's fault!" Erik shouted. "The dog's face was all full of porcupine quills and she couldn't eat or anything. She needed help, and Dr. Bob came—"

Big Darrell's eyes narrowed at this, and Erik hurried to add, "He didn't even charge us anything because he's a nice guy and he just wanted to help her."

Not like you. The unspoken words hung in the air. If Big Darrell sensed them, he showed no sign.

"Quill, come," Erik said. He couldn't stand watching her standing at Big Darrell's feet, wagging her tail and sniffing his boots, waiting for a pat that wasn't going to come. When she returned to stand beside him, Erik reached down to rub her head. Then he stepped forward, placing himself between Quill and Big Darrell.

He tried to keep his voice even, although his hands were shaking and his heart was drumming a jerky rhythm in his chest. "Oma told me you said no more dogs. It's only until Dr. Bob finds the owner. And I've got money. If there's any charge, I'll pay for everything."

There was silence for a while. Finally, Big Darrell heaved an angry sigh and said, "It's too late to do anything with it tonight. It can stay until tomorrow. No longer."

"Oh, Darrell, that's wonderful. Isn't it, Erik?" Oma asked softly.

Erik didn't answer. He was afraid that if he opened his mouth he'd say what he was thinking, which was that there was no way he was going to thank Big Darrell and act all grateful because the man had said Quill could stay one lousy night in his lousy house.

He and Big Darrell continued to stare at each other. Finally Big Darrell spoke. "You called it a name."

"*Her*, not *it*."

Big Darrell said impatiently, "How did you know its name?"

"I just made it up," Erik answered, wondering what the man was getting at.

Big Darrell shook his head slowly, a disgusted expression on his face. Erik had to force himself not to look away from the man's icy blue gaze.

"No sense in giving a name to what's not yours to keep," Big Darrell muttered. "Now take that mutt out to the barn."

"If she's sleeping in the barn, then I am, too," Erik answered.

"Oh, Erik—" Oma began, looking distressed.

But Big Darrell interrupted, saying, "Suit yourself." He went into the kitchen, where he sat down and began to silently eat his supper.

Oma gave Erik a weak smile and gently touched his shoulder. "I'll talk to him," she said.

Erik could hear the fear and reluctance in her

voice. "No," he said. "Don't bother. I'll be fine." He bit his tongue to keep from saying what he wanted to say: *I'd rather sleep out than in the same house with him, any day.*

"Erik," said Oma, almost in a whisper. "Won't you—"

"I *want* to sleep in the barn. With Quill."

Oma sighed, her distress evident in her face. "Wait, then." She took a flashlight from a shelf by the door. "You'll need this. And a pillow and some more blankets for yourself."

"I'll get them off my bed," Erik replied, and headed for the stairs. He hastily removed his bedding and put on a sweatshirt. Back in the living room, he picked up Quill's blanket. Arms full, he turned to face Oma, who appeared close to tears.

"I wish you'd stay inside," she said. "He—"

"I'm sleeping in the barn, Oma. It's *okay*. Really."

His grandmother reached up and fussed with the neck of his sweatshirt. Then, with a brave attempt at a smile, she said, "Good night, then. And—sleep well."

"'Night," Erik said, and escaped gratefully into the darkness.

Oma turned on the porch light as he and Quill walked toward the barn. Once inside, he found the hay bales, spread out his blankets and Quill's, plumped his pillow, and stretched out with Quill beside him. He buried his flushed and angry face in the warm fur of her neck.

For a long time, he lay awake, his hands curling into fists at his sides as he thought about Big Darrell. *What's his problem, anyway? What did I ever do to him? Him and all his stupid rules. "Don't go in that room. Didn't I say no dogs? No sense in naming something that's not yours." I don't know how Oma can stand living here alone with him. There's no way I can take it for six months. I won't make it one more day in that house.*

The instant he stopped thinking about Big Darrell, he worried that Dr. Bob would call at any moment, having found Quill's owner. He tried to think of some way, any way, to keep her, but there was no solution, not as long as he lived under Big Darrell's roof.

10

In the morning, Erik lay awake, dreading having to see Big Darrell. To his relief, he heard the kitchen door shut, followed by the sound of the truck starting up. He got up and watched from the barn as Big Darrell drove off. Evidently the beet harvest continued, even on Sunday, and Erik was glad of it.

When he walked into the house, Oma made a big to-do over him and Quill, asking how they'd slept and what they'd like for breakfast.

"Eggs would be great," Erik said. "Please."

"Erik," Oma said softly, "you musn't mind Big Darrell. He—has a lot on his mind."

Erik was still too angry to answer, even if he could have thought of something to say to that.

She continued apologetically, "He called this

morning. Dr. Bob is going to come for the—for Quill—later today."

Erik felt his jaw clench in fury.

Oma blinked, looking as helpless as he felt. "I'm sorry," she whispered.

After a long silence, she sighed and looked down at Quill, who was sitting by Erik's feet. "Now what on earth are we going to feed *you* this morning?" she asked. "I guess it'll have to be ham and eggs for you and Erik both, how does that sound?"

Quill thumped her tail. As Oma busied herself cooking, Erik examined Quill's face. There was a little swelling, but it wasn't bad at all, and she seemed to be acting just fine.

Oma handed Erik a plate of fried eggs, cooked crispy on the edges the way he liked them. She told him she was going to church and asked if he wanted to come along.

"I'll just stay here. Dr. Bob's coming, remember?" he said bitterly. He reached for his fork and began to eat, barely tasting the food.

Oma broke several more eggs over the remaining ham and toast, and placed the dish on the floor for Quill. "Well, my friend will be coming for me soon," said Oma, "so I'd better get ready." After a moment, she said suddenly, "I suppose you think I'm silly not to drive."

Erik, surprised, looked up.

Her eyes were shiny with tears again as she said, "I used to. But I stopped after"—she hesitated for a moment, wide-eyed, then plunged ahead—"well, I stopped after we lost *Dan*." She paused again, then took a deep breath. "There. I said it."

Erik licked his lips and swallowed uneasily, not knowing what to say.

"Did your mother tell you about your uncle Dan?" Oma asked.

He nodded. Quill, maybe sensing the tension in the room, came over and placed her head in his lap. He stroked her ears as Oma continued.

"After we got the news about Dan, I had two accidents in the car in one week. I couldn't even say how they happened. I don't know where my mind was. I haven't trusted myself to drive since then. And now it's been so long, thirty-four years, I can scarcely believe it . . ." Her voice trailed off.

She looked so small right then, and so forlorn, Erik hurried to say, "I don't think you're silly, Oma."

"Thank you, Erik." She smiled wanly and added, "I expect Big Darrell does."

Erik wanted to tell her he didn't care what Big Darrell thought, but he kept silent. Big Darrell was her husband, after all. And Erik kept having the feeling there were things happening that he didn't understand.

"It felt good to say Dan's name out loud just now," Oma said. "I say it all the time in my prayers, of course. But Big Darrell doesn't like me to talk about Dan." Her voice low, she added, "He stopped going to church after Dan died. He doesn't pray. He says—he says the God who allowed his son to die is dead to him." She looked at Erik with eyes full of sorrow, and whispered, "Poor Darrell."

This confused Erik even further. *Poor Darrell?* he thought. Was she crazy? To hide his discomfort, he got up and took his empty plate to the sink to wash it, and was relieved when Oma said she was going upstairs to get dressed for church.

Erik took Quill outside, unable to sit in that sad kitchen for one more moment. Angrily, he picked up a stick and threw it as hard as he could. Quill chased it, picked it up, ran back to his side, and sat. When Erik held out his hand, she very gently opened her mouth and allowed him to take it.

A wave of affection and regret swept through Erik,

and he dropped to his knees to hold Quill's smooth ears and put his face to hers. How could he stand to give her up?

Oma's friend pulled into the driveway, and Oma came outside dressed for church. "There's a coffee hour after the service," she told Erik, "and I'm on the cleanup committee afterwards. Then Rosemary and I have more decorating to do for the Harvest Festival. So I'll be gone until, oh, about two o'clock or so. Are you sure you'll be all right?"

"I'll be fine," Erik told her.

She looked as if she might be about to say more. Then she gave her head a quick little shake and said, "Okay, then. I'll see you after church."

She waved as the car pulled away, and Erik waved back halfheartedly.

As if to remind him of what they were supposed to be doing, Quill threw the stick for herself by tossing her head to send it flying. Erik could have sworn she grinned at him before she ran after it.

It was almost impossible to remain grouchy when Quill was so rambunctious and cheerful, but the reality of Erik's situation was beginning to sink in—hard. It was Sunday. Dr. Bob was coming soon to take Quill. Maybe, just maybe, he'd have been able to stand being here if he had Quill to keep him company. But without her? All he had to look forward to was starting at a new school, where he didn't know anybody and had no friends. Everything about Fortuna, North Dakota, seemed strange and foreign, and Erik had every reason to think the kids would be different, too. What if all the guys were as weird and unfriendly as Big Darrell?

He thought about what Oma had said about Big Darrell and Dan, and his mind returned to the bedroom at the top of the stairs. He decided to go back and look around some more. He didn't know what, exactly, he hoped to learn. Mostly, he was curious. Dan *was* his uncle, after all.

"Come on, Quill," he called.

In Dan's room, he studied the photograph on the wall. Dan gazed into the camera, looking handsome and very young. *Way too young to be dead,* Erik couldn't help thinking. Also, he had the feeling that Dan's serious, businesslike expression was put on, as if the normally smiling, happy-go-lucky boy thought this was the way a soldier *ought* to look in his official military picture.

Next, Erik examined the medal. He hadn't ever seen a Purple Heart before, but knew this had to be one. Oma and Big Darrell must have been given the decoration after Dan was killed in action.

Wanting to know more about Dan than the bare facts revealed by the flag and the medal and the photo, Erik opened the top dresser drawer. It contained report cards, some photos of Dan in his football uniform, and some 4-H ribbons like the ones on the mirror in his mother's old bedroom. The next two drawers held neatly folded clothes: T-shirts and underwear and jeans.

He wandered over to the closet. There were several stiff, pressed army uniforms hanging there, a camouflage jacket, and some denim and flannel shirts. Shoes were neatly lined up in a row on the floor: shiny, polished army boots, a pair of hunting boots, a pair of loafers, and some sneakers.

The shininess of the boots caught Erik's attention. There was no dust on them—or on anything in the room. *After thirty-four years?* he wondered. Then he realized that someone—Oma, of course, it had to be—must come in here to clean. He pictured her lovingly dusting Dan's things, and maybe saying his name out loud, when Big Darrell wasn't home. It made him sad to think of it.

On the overhead shelf in the closet was some

camping stuff: a sleeping bag, a canteen, and a canvas sack with a shoulder strap that he recognized as a Boy Scout mess kit. Next to these things was a shoebox tied with a piece of twine. He reached for it and slipped off the twine. Inside was a dog collar, a leash, a couple of long tail feathers from a pheasant, and more photos of Dan with a yellow Labrador retriever. In some, the dog was a puppy and Dan was about Erik's age. One, labeled "Elvis—4-H Obedience School graduate!" showed Dan holding up a certificate and laughing as the dog's tongue bathed his face. Flipping through them, Erik could see the boy and the dog growing up together.

Several photos were paper-clipped together. The one on top was of Dan and Big Darrell, both dressed for hunting and holding shotguns. They stood beside Elvis, who held a male pheasant in his mouth. Dan and Big Darrell were both grinning like fools, and even Elvis seemed to be smiling proudly as he held his prize.

The next, clearly taken on the same golden fall day, showed Dan and Big Darrell kneeling beside Elvis in the fallen leaves. Dan held up a bird in each hand. Big Darrell had one arm around Dan and the other around Elvis's neck. Once again, they all looked deliriously happy.

A third showed Oma, Big Darrell, and Dan sitting at the table, with Dan holding a carving knife and fork over a platter of roasted birds. Elvis stood by Dan. Everybody was giving a big, cheesy smile to the picture-taker, who Erik figured had been his mom.

As he studied the pictures, a fierce longing rose inside him. It was as if a lot of things he'd read and dreamed about and half imagined suddenly came into focus. He wanted to *be* the boy in those photographs, or to be like him, at least. In the photos Erik saw everything he had tried to explain to his mother about wanting to go hunting, plus something else he hadn't understood at the time: how a big part of the experience was sharing it with a dog.

Erik had listened to Patrick and his dad talking about what a great dog Hot Spots was, and how amazing she was at finding birds. But he hadn't actually hunted with her. Looking at Dan and Elvis, he imagined them in the field, working together, combining their skill and knowledge and instincts in the hunt. He wanted to have that experience, with Quill.

Along with all these thoughts and feelings, the photos raised even more questions about Big Darrell. It was impossible to believe that the casually affectionate man smiling in the pictures, with his arm around Elvis and Dan, was the same stern, grim-faced person Erik had met. The one who didn't hunt, who seemed to hate kids—well, Erik, anyway—the one who had said, "What's that dog doing in here?" And "Didn't I say *no more dogs*?" And "The dog goes."

It didn't make sense. With a sigh, Erik retied the twine around the box. As he reached up to return it to the shelf, he caught a glimpse of something leaning against the back wall of the closet. Pushing the hanging clothing to the side, he bent down and pulled out a twelve-gauge, semiautomatic shotgun.

"Wow," he murmured.

He recognized the gun immediately as the same one Dan had been holding in the photographs. Stacked against the rear wall of the closet were several boxes of shotgun shells.

Quill, who had been sitting in a patch of sunlight by the window, came over and sniffed the gun with interest.

"You know what this is, don't you, Quill?" Erik asked.

He didn't think Oma would leave a loaded gun around the house, but he checked it to be sure.

Pointing the muzzle toward the floor and keeping his fingers well away from the trigger, he pulled back the bolt. No cartridge popped out of the chamber, but he pulled the bolt a couple more times to make sure there weren't any shells in the magazine, either.

He noticed a metal plate on the wooden stock, engraved with a scene of a man standing, gun to his shoulder, over a dog on point. The dog stood with its tail straight out, front paw lifted, staring with great focus at a pheasant that was hiding in the brush. The dog looked an awful lot like Quill. Whoever the artist was, he was really good. Erik could almost see the dog quivering with contained excitement.

Quill watched him as he hefted the gun, testing the length and weight of it. It felt good. He liked the smell of gun oil and the faint odor of gunpowder that clung to it. He lifted it to his shoulder, and was sighting down the barrel when the phone rang.

He froze for a moment. A rush of guilt flooded through him, guilt at being caught snooping in Dan's room and handling Dan's gun. He felt this even as he realized it was silly: whoever was on the phone couldn't see him.

The guilt passed, followed by dread. He was pretty

sure he knew who was calling. He forced himself to set the gun down and walk to Oma and Big Darrell's room.

When he picked up the receiver, Dr. Bob's voice boomed, "Erik, good news! I found the dog's owner."

11

Erik's heart leaped, then sank as Dr. Bob continued talking.

"It's a fella by the name of Mike Duvochin. He lives down near Bismarck. He brought some of his dogs up this way last weekend to hunt sharp-tails, just the way I figured. And this pup took off on him. Says he called and whistled and drove around looking for her, but finally he had to leave."

"He just left Quill behind?" Erik asked incredulously.

"Who? Oh, is that what you're calling her?" Dr. Bob chuckled. "Cute. Anyway, Duvochin said it was getting dark and he couldn't spend all night looking. He had to get home. He didn't know anything about the porcupine. He can't come today, but thinks he'll be able to get up this way tomorrow or the next day."

"Oh," Erik said weakly.

"How's the dog doing?"

Erik looked at Quill, who was over in the corner sniffing a pair of Oma's slippers, and smiled despite himself. "Great," he said. "She acts like nothing ever happened."

"That's the beauty of dogs," Dr. Bob said. "They don't dwell on the past. Any swelling?"

"Maybe just a little."

"Is she eating?"

"Venison, ham, and eggs, so far," Erik told him.

Dr. Bob laughed and said, "Nothing but the best, huh? Well, listen, it's no problem for me to keep her until Duvochin can come for her. But it doesn't look as if I'll be able to get there until maybe six o'clock. Is that going to be soon enough for Big Darrell?"

Erik thought about the way his grandfather's cold blue eyes had flattened when he first saw Quill, and the look on his face when he said, "Take that mutt out to the barn."

"I guess it'll have to be," he said.

"All right, then. I'll see you tonight."

Erik forced himself to say thanks before hanging

up. Quill, who was curled on the rug next to the bed, got to her feet and came over to him. Erik took her head in his hands, and they looked into each other's eyes.

Dr. Bob's call made it final. Even if, by some miracle, Big Darrell had relented and let Quill stay another night, she was going back to her owner. He thought about Quill returning to this Duvochin guy, who obviously didn't care about her anywhere near as much as Erik did, or he'd never have left her behind to contend with a porcupine all on her own.

He thought about going to school the next day, a prospect daunting in itself. Then he imagined coming home at the end of the day to this sagging, unhappy house. Oma was nice, he had to admit, and he felt how hard she was trying to make him feel at home. But any welcoming warmth she created was blotted out by the dark, ominous presence of Big Darrell.

He couldn't stand it.

And suddenly a plan came to him, breathtaking in its perfection and simplicity. He would leave, and take Quill with him.

He had a shotgun, and shells. He had Quill. They would live off the land together. After all, they were in a place where one could hardly "swing a dead cat" without hitting a pheasant, a place where birds and deer

and jackrabbits were more plentiful than human be-
ings. And while the land was empty of people, it was
full of places to hide. No one would ever find them if
they didn't wish to be found.

Big Darrell would be positively thrilled—if Big
Darrell was ever actually thrilled about anything—to
find them gone. Erik hesitated when he thought about
Oma, remembering her pleased expression when he'd
hugged her and the feel of her hands on his back when
she had hugged him in return. But he was sure that
his being there only made her life with Big Darrell
harder.

He thought of his parents, halfway across the
world. *They're the ones who sent me here and said to make
the best of it. And that's what I'm doing,* he told himself.

He glanced at the clock on Oma's bedside table. It
was a few minutes before nine. That gave him plenty
of time for a good head start in case anyone came
looking for him.

He thought about what he'd need to take with
him. His mother had told him about how crazy and
extreme the weather in North Dakota could be. He
wasn't one hundred percent sure he believed that
she had gotten badly burned while sunbathing one

morning and frostbitten later the same afternoon, or that she used to watch the whitecaps in Oma's birdbath, but he gathered up all his warmest clothes, including rain gear, and stuffed them into his backpack. He added his wallet but left his cell phone on the dresser. It was useless here, and there was no one he wanted to call. He and Quill were going to make it on their own. Kids in pioneer days didn't have phones.

He grabbed his toothbrush from the bathroom and headed back to Dan's room. The shotgun shells went into the pack. Next he tied the old camping mess kit and the canteen onto the outside of the pack by their straps. From the box he took Elvis's collar, which he placed around Quill's neck, and the leash, which he used to lash the sleeping bag to the bottom of the pack.

He was putting on the camouflage jacket when Dan's hunting boots caught his eye. They looked sturdier than his own hiking boots, so he decided to try them on. They were a little roomy, but not bad at all when he put on two pairs of thick wool socks from Dan's drawer.

He picked up the gun, closed the closet door, and surveyed the room. There was no obvious sign that he'd been here. Oma or Big Darrell would have to come in and look in the closet to notice anything was missing, and somehow he doubted they would suspect right away that he'd been in Dan's room. Carefully, he closed the door behind him and went downstairs, Quill at his heels.

In the kitchen he gathered a big box of matches, which he put in a plastic baggie, and a couple of larger plastic bags for keeping his gear dry in case of rain. Opening cabinets and pulling out drawers, he looked for other things he might need and found a Swiss Army knife and another, longer knife.

He and Quill would hunt for their food, of course. But just to be on the safe side, he raided the refrigerator for some cheese, a package of bologna, and two apples. From the pantry he took a pack of cookies, the remains of a loaf of bread, a nearly full jar of peanut butter, and a box of crackers. Then he filled the canteen with water.

Looking around the kitchen, he couldn't think of anything he was forgetting. His eyes fell on the notepad and pen sitting by the telephone. He imagined Oma coming home from church to find him gone. He remembered her saying to Dr. Bob, "I can't have anything happening to Erik. He's my daughter Darlene's boy, you know."

On the notepad he wrote, "Dear Oma, Quill and I went for a walk, so I packed a lunch. Dr. Bob is coming by for her around 6." He read it over. It implied—without actually saying—that he and Quill planned to be back in time to meet Dr. Bob. Nothing he'd written was an outright lie. He and Quill *were* going for a walk. He just hoped the note would buy them some extra time. He signed it, "Your grandson, Erik."

Hoisting his pack onto his back, he called to Quill. Together, they headed out into the wide and windy prairie.

12

The sun shone brightly in the cloudless sky, and Erik shaded his eyes against the glare. As he looked around at the miles of unpopulated countryside stretching as far as he could see, a feeling of exhilaration rose in him. From this moment on, he realized, every decision was his to make. Not only that, these were going to be *real* decisions, important ones, having to do with staying alive. He had one simple job, he told himself, to live off the land.

The challenge quickened his blood.

First decision: which way to go?

He adjusted the pack on his back, shouldered the shotgun, and called to Quill, who seemed to have caught the scent of his excitement and was racing happily across the driveway toward the road. When she returned, he explained to her that they would be staying away from roads, crossing them only when necessary and when they were certain they wouldn't be seen. This wasn't nearly as difficult as it would have been back home, because the roads out here were few and far between. He'd noticed that, for the most part, they ran north to south and east to west, dividing the land into huge blocks that were several miles long on every side. That made a lot of space in which a boy and a dog could disappear. Also, in those wide-open spaces he could see or hear a car coming miles before it got close enough to worry about.

First, he decided, they would head for the cover of the line of trees he had spotted the night he arrived. From the car, the land had appeared flat and empty to him. But now, as he moved across it on foot, it told a different story. There were subtle dips and gentle mounds in the earth, and places where the rain had washed deep ditches. There were low spots where cattails and brush grew around the edges of little ponds, called potholes.

At home, that meant a hole in the road that caused the car to lurch and his father to say bad words. But his mom had told him about prairie potholes, which were rounded depressions in the earth that had been left behind by glaciers. Nowadays they held rainwater and snowmelt. Some of them were the size of a back-yard swimming pool, others as far across as a football field.

There were patches of scrubby trees and small stands of woods, and gullies and ravines. There were odd objects people had left behind: rusty farm implements, an old watering trough, the foundation of a building long gone, a pile of rocks cleared from a field. Erik noted with satisfaction that all of these provided cover where he and Quill could hide, if need be. He imagined that pheasant and deer hid in those same kinds of places.

Erik was also pleased to see that Quill, with her mottled coat, blended in well with the rocks and dirt and grass, and he congratulated himself on his own clothing: faded jeans, a gray T-shirt, Dan's camo jacket, and his own favorite camo-print baseball cap.

When they reached the trees, he turned to the south. He didn't have a compass, but he'd noticed where the sun had come up the past two mornings, and where it had set, so he knew which way was south.

He figured they'd move carefully, far from the eyes of anyone driving on the road, and use this first day to put as much distance as they could between themselves and his grandparents' farmhouse. He chose south as their direction because he knew that Canada wasn't far to the north. Back in New York, when he'd gone to Canada with his parents for a weekend vacation, they had crossed a big bridge where they'd had to show their passports to the guards and answer questions about where they were born and what they were planning to do in Canada. He didn't know what the border was like out here, but he wasn't taking the chance of being spotted or questioned.

When Erik looked back, his grandparents' house was already no more than a speck in the distance. A V of geese flew high overhead, honking urgently to one another, reminding Erik of the question framed in the picture his mother had drawn. He had found the answer. *This*, he felt sure, was how he was meant to live his one wild life: with his gun on his shoulder and his dog by his side, free to go where he pleased in a wide and wild place, with no grownups to give orders and hold him back. He had only the supplies he could fit in his pack and his own wits and courage, and that was all he needed.

13

When they were safely out of sight of the road and the farmhouse, Erik began to relax a little. He'd been so busy with his own thoughts that he hadn't been paying attention to what Quill was doing. Now he realized that Quill wasn't just ambling along in front of him.

She was hunting.

With her nose to the ground, she raced along until she caught an interesting scent that either halted her in her tracks for further investigation or sent her off in a new direction. Sometimes she stopped, lifted her head, sniffed the air, and chased after a scent borne by the breeze.

Erik knew that his puny human nose was at least a million times less discriminating than Quill's, which was why he had no idea what the tantalizing odors were that were riveting her attention. But he found it fascinating to watch her.

She was running along the border between a brushy hedgerow and a field of wheat stubble. The grain had already been harvested, but a fair number of wheat kernels had been left behind on the ground. Suddenly Quill's body became tense, her attention more focused. Her tail, which had been wagging happily, began to beat back and forth so quickly it was almost a blur. Then she made a quarter turn and slammed to an absolute standstill. Her gaze was fixed straight ahead, at the hedgerow. Her tail stood out horizontal and motionless now, and her right paw was lifted as if she'd been asked to "shake." She looked exactly like the etching on Dan's gun.

Quill was on point!

Erik was so entranced by her performance that for a full minute he just stood, watching. Quill's concentration never wavered. Erik scanned the brush where the dog's gaze was pinned. For the life of him, he couldn't see anything but grass and browning weeds. Time stood still in the warm, quiet air.

"What is it, girl?" he whispered. "Is something

there?" He took a tentative step forward. Quill looked over at him for one split second, an expression on her face that seemed to say, "You smell that, too, right? Are you ready?"

And—*pptttttrrrrrrrr!* In a flurry of wings, a pheasant rose into the air, cackling in outrage. It seemed to hang in the air for a moment. Even if its roosterlike cry hadn't given it away as a male, Erik got a clear look at its long trailing tail feathers and the gleam of green, red, and white on its head. It flew swiftly into the far distance and out of sight, leaving a single white dropping as a protest.

Erik was so startled he nearly lost hold of his gun. He gasped and watched as the bird disappeared. Quill had flinched slightly and taken a few steps when the bird first took off, but now she was back on point.

"It's gone, girl," said Erik when he had recovered from his surprise.

Quill ignored him.

"That was a great point, Quill, but the bird's gone. It flew away."

Quill continued to stare into the hedgerow, her paw lifted and her entire body quivering. Erik moved closer to her, wondering if there was a command he was supposed to give to release her. Hadn't she seen the bird fly? How long would she stay like this? What was she doing?

"Quill," he began, and, at that moment, a hen pheasant—then two, then *three, seven, ten more!*—broke from the cover of the hedgerow. Smaller than the male, dull brown in color, and silent except for the furious whirr of their wingbeats, they flew off in all directions.

Erik's amazement was quickly followed by dismay. *Some hunter you are,* he thought. *Your gun wasn't even loaded.* Even if it had been, he'd been utterly unprepared when the birds had flown. Worse, he'd doubted Quill, who, unlike him, seemed to know exactly what she was doing.

"I'm sorry, girl," he said, bending down to give her a pat. "From now on, I promise I'll try to hold up my end. Beginning with"—he grimaced to himself—"loading my gun."

He put shells in the chamber and put the safety on, wishing he'd had a chance to go hunting, even just *once,* with Mr. Holt and Hot Spots, in order to get a little experience. As it was, he would have to learn from Quill and the birds themselves. What had they just taught him?

Quill had clearly been saying, "Watch me! Stick with me! I'll tell you where the birds are!" All Erik had to do was pay attention. It was almost as if the dog had performed a magic trick, conjuring pheasants out of thin air. Without Quill, Erik would have walked right by them, never suspecting they were there.

As for the birds, the rooster had flown solo, before the hens. If that was usually the case, it was important information to know. Hunters were only allowed to shoot roosters, not hens. If the males were generally the ones to spook and fly first, he'd have to stay on his toes.

He wondered what the birds had been doing when Quill pointed them. Had they been just hanging around in the hedgerow enjoying the nice day? Somehow, Erik doubted it.

He looked about in the wheat field and saw some more pheasant poop, as well as several tracks left in low spots where the earth was smooth and damp. Erik guessed they had been eating the grain that had been left behind on the ground. Since the wheat stubble was only about four inches high, they would be easy for a predator to spot. He figured that when they'd seen him and Quill approaching, they'd scuttled over to the hedgerow to hide.

If he was right, it was another important piece of information. He'd remember to keep his eye out for fields like this one.

Erik was about to move on when he realized he was hungry and thirsty. He didn't have a watch—*who needed a watch, anyway? A pioneer boy would know how to tell time by the sun*—but he thought they'd been walking for about two hours.

He tipped the canteen up and let the water run down his parched throat. Quill watched him, her tongue hanging out, panting. He quickly poured the rest of the water into the lid of the mess kit, which doubled as a bowl, and she drank. When the water was gone, she looked up, still panting thirstily.

Earlier, he'd seen her take a long drink from a medium-sized pothole. The water, which was brown with green algae around the edges, had looked disgusting to Erik, but Quill hadn't seemed to mind it in the least.

The pothole was far behind them, though, and he would need to find water for her, and for himself, too, pretty soon. He was going to have to plan ahead and boil water to fill his canteen each morning. That meant he was going to have to camp near water. Okay, good, that would be part of his plan from here on.

He took the food from his pack and made two bologna and cheese sandwiches. Quill devoured hers in two seconds flat, but Erik took his time, savoring the flavor, thinking that never before in his life had a bologna and cheese sandwich tasted quite so fine. He and Quill each had a cookie, then Erik ate one of the apples. To his surprise, Quill eagerly chewed up the core.

The food he had brought wasn't going to last long, though, not with two of them eating. They had enough for dinner that night, and for breakfast and possibly lunch the next day. But very soon he and Quill were going to have to find some more game. And he was going to have to shoot it.

That made him wonder: When he did actually shoot something, would someone hear the noise and come to investigate? Just as this new worry entered his mind, he heard the sound of a faraway gunshot, then another and another. He remembered Dr. Bob saying that the season was open for sharp-tailed grouse as well as pheasant. For all Erik knew, it was open season for deer, squirrels, rabbits, ducks, and geese, too. That meant other hunters would be shooting, not just him. People would be used to the sound and probably wouldn't pay much attention.

That was good because he was going to be hunting illegally. He didn't have a North Dakota license.

Well, there was nothing he could do about that. He and Quill had to eat. And, anyway, he didn't intend to get caught.

14

When they came to their first paved road, Erik called Quill back to him and approached carefully. After making sure there was no sign of a vehicle coming from either direction, they crossed and moved quickly into the big field on the other side. Erik felt uncomfortably exposed in such open territory and kept an eye out, prepared to drop to the ground and lie flat if someone drove by. No one did.

He didn't know exactly what time it was, but he didn't think Oma would even have gotten home from church. No one would be thinking of looking for him yet. But if and when people began searching, he didn't want anyone to remember seeing a boy and a brown-and-white-speckled dog crossing this road or any other. If and when they looked for him, they'd have to look in all directions, and he and Quill had only gone in one. Also, he imagined, if they did search for him, they'd likely assume that he'd gotten lost and *wanted* to be found. They wouldn't expect him to be purposely eluding them.

As he and Quill traveled through the afternoon, Quill went on point three more times. Each time a group of birds flew, with the roosters flushing first and the hens holding a bit longer. Erik shot each time, *blam blam blam blam blam*, emptying the chamber of all five shells, but hitting nothing.

The first two times, Quill raced around, searching in all directions for the downed birds. When there were no birds for her to retrieve, she seemed confused. When no birds fell the third time, either, she glanced over her shoulder at Erik with mild reproof.

"I'm sorry, girl," he said miserably. "It's not your fault."

Real hunting was turning out to be quite a bit different from shooting clay targets, and he was getting worried. Each box of shells held twenty-five cartridges, and he only had four boxes. He'd just shot off fifteen, and he had nothing to show for it. If he didn't improve his aim—and fast—he and Quill would be in big trouble. He had his wallet containing his allowance money, but he didn't want to risk going into a store.

A sudden exhaustion overcame him. With it came a whisper of fear that he had made a huge mistake.

This last thought made him even more disappointed in himself. What kind of wimp was he, anyway? He'd been out on his own for less than a day. Some pioneer.

He tried to recall what advice Mr. Holt had given him when they'd been at the target range. *Use your front hand to start the muzzle moving in the direction of the target. Then swing at the same time you bring the stock up and mount it near your face. When the bird is moving, you can't stop your swing to shoot at it. You have to come from behind the bird, swing your gun past it, and shoot ahead of it.*

That was what he'd been doing wrong, he realized. He'd stopped his motion when he took his shots. What else had Mr. Holt said? *Plan with your head, then shoot from your heart. Do your thinking before you pull the trigger. Your eyes will never lie to your hands.* When he'd said that, Erik didn't get it. But now he thought maybe he did. He just had to relax and remember what he already knew. He'd do better next time. Squaring his shoulders, he shook off his trepidation.

Quill, as if reading his mind, shook herself all over, too. Then she looked at him with an eager doggy grin and ran ahead. As far as she was concerned, the missed shots were forgotten and she was ready to move on. Erik couldn't help but grin back. Some of the confidence and excitement he'd felt upon starting out that morning returned to him.

The next time he checked, the sun had moved far to the west. Although it still looked fairly high in the sky, Erik knew that when it started to drop, darkness would fall quickly. He was becoming seriously concerned about Quill. Her tongue lolled like a long, thick, pink balloon, and she was panting heavily. Her pace, which hadn't wavered all day long, was slowing, and her rear legs looked wobbly. Her eager expression was gone, her eyes glazed. When Erik felt her nose, it was hot and dry.

He was beginning to panic about finding water when they came over a rise and he saw a barn in the distance, with what looked like a fenced-in corral by its side. He headed toward it. A dirt drive led to the barn from a side road too far away for Erik to see. There was an old red gas pump, but the only vehicle in sight was a rusted-out truck with no tires. It seemed safe to approach.

In the corral was an aluminum watering trough with a spigot above it. Erik went over to inspect it and couldn't believe his luck when the handle turned and rusty brown water poured out. After a while, it began to clear. He took off his pack, filled the bowl-like lid of the mess kit, and set it on the ground for Quill. She drank greedily. He refilled the bowl two more times before she stopped and lay down, tongue dripping. She was still panting, but she already seemed much better. He gave her a quick hug before filling his canteen and taking a long drink himself.

Thirst slaked, he took a look around. He could almost believe he was the only human being on earth, certainly the only one for miles in any direction. Although someone obviously owned the property, there were no animals in the barn or corral and there seemed no reason for anybody to come out here tonight.

He walked around to the far side of the barn and decided it was a good place to make camp. After spreading one of the large plastic bags on the ground, he unrolled his sleeping bag and tried to get Quill to lie on it while he collected wood for a fire. But she refused to leave his side. She even picked up a stick and carried it, dropping it on the pile Erik collected, as if she knew what he was doing. He laughed, shaking his head and telling her, for perhaps the twentieth time that day, what a good, smart dog she was.

When the fire was going, he made four thin sandwiches with the rest of the bologna and cheese. Quill gulped hers down as before, but once again Erik took his time, watching as the flames licked at the wood and the sky grew dark. He was still hungry, but he told himself that tomorrow he would hunt successfully, then cook and eat his fill of his very first game dinner.

All day he'd pushed from his mind any thoughts about what might be happening back at his grandparents' farmhouse. But they crowded in now that it was growing dark. Big Darrell was probably home, and Dr. Bob would have come for Quill by now. They would have no inkling that he had run away, but were undoubtedly concerned that he'd gotten lost.

He pictured Oma out in the yard, anxiously scanning the deepening shadows for a glimpse of him. He imagined her coming back inside, perhaps asking Big Darrell what to do. He saw Big Darrell sitting stone-faced in front of the snowy television screen, saying gruffly, "Boy'll come back when he's scared and hungry."

That's where you're wrong, thought Erik.

A group of pheasants landed in the overgrown field to the east of them. Erik listened as they called to one another, gathering together for protection in the deep cover.

Ducks and geese whistled and honked softly as they flew over on their way to seek their own refuge for the night. Erik pictured the change that was taking place all around him as the creatures of the day sought sleep, giving the prairie over to those that preferred the nighttime: owls, deer, skunks, bats, raccoons, opossums, and—

An eerie call filled the darkness, a mix of yips and barks ending in what almost sounded like the high-pitched scream of a person in pain. This call was followed by another and another and another, then all the voices joined together in a chorus—*Yip-yip-AAARROOOOOOOOO*—before fading into silence. Coyotes! Thrilled, Erik felt the hairs on the back of his neck rise, as Quill stood and looked about, whining fretfully.

"It's okay, girl," Erik whispered. "Coyotes don't mess with dogs or people." After a moment he added, "I'm sure of that." After another moment he murmured, "Pretty sure, anyway."

Quill lay down beside him and curled up with her

nose to her tail. Erik added sticks to the fire, breathing in its smoky tang, feeling its comforting warmth, watching as it hungrily devoured his offerings. From time to time he glanced upward, where stars were beginning to dot the sky in numbers he never saw back home. Quill let out a loud sigh and settled her head in Erik's lap. He stroked her head, his hands moving gently over her closed eyes.

When there was nothing left of the fire but a few embers, he wriggled down in his sleeping bag and closed his eyes, too. Quill snored lightly beside him, but Erik couldn't sleep. From time to time the coyotes howled, calling each other to the hunt. Bats swooped overhead in erratic flight, chasing insects, their squeaky chirps barely audible. Over and over again, an owl gave its mournful call: *Hoo, hoo-hoo, hoo, hoo.* Then it stopped, and in the sudden hush, Erik heard the whisper of wing beats, followed by a rustle in the grass and the squeak of a small rodent.

The night was full of the sounds and movements of other nocturnal creatures Erik could only guess at. There were times when the noises in the dark sounded awfully close. Sometimes it seemed that whatever was making them had to be very big. But Erik wasn't afraid, and it wasn't apprehension that kept him awake. He'd never felt quite so alive, and he didn't want to miss anything on this first night of his new life.

A chill fell as the day's heat rose and disappeared into the clear, starry sky. Erik was profoundly grateful for the warmth of Quill's body and the comfort of her company. Alone out here, he might have been overwhelmed by the hugeness of the prairie. He might have felt defeated by his own smallness in the face of it. But with Quill, he felt anchored to the earth, part of it all.

15

Erik must have slept finally, because he awoke to find Quill standing over him, her cool, wet nose nudging his face. She appeared to be fully refreshed after her night's sleep and ready to *go*.

Erik sat up and looked around at the sun rising pink and new, illuminating the ragged wisps of mist that hovered over the land. In the distance he could see a deer walking cautiously along a line of trees, looking for a place to bed down during the heat of the day. Off to the west somewhere, a pheasant cackled. Now that he was learning to look and to listen, this place that had at first appeared lifeless to him was bustling with activity.

He and Quill had to get moving, too. They couldn't risk staying in one place too long. And they had to keep moving steadily farther from where they'd started, in the event that a search party had been called out.

From his pack, Erik took out peanut butter and crackers for breakfast. He smeared peanut butter on a cracker and handed it to Quill. Too late, he realized this was a mistake. The peanut butter stuck the cracker to the roof of her mouth. Looking embarrassed, she smacked her tongue again and again, trying to get it loose. Erik choked back his laughter and made little sandwiches, with the peanut butter inside the crackers, after that. Soon they had emptied the jar and finished the crackers, and after Erik ate the last apple, Quill crunched happily through the core.

His stomach still felt empty, and he spent a moment recalling the eggs Oma had fried for him the morning before, their edges crispy, and the ham, salty and chewy, and the toast, dripping with butter and topped with raspberry jam . . . He pushed himself to his feet. Enough of that. It was time to pack up and go, time to find his own food.

It was then that he made the discovery that it is impossible to get a dog to drink if she doesn't feel like it. He filled the bowl with water for Quill, but she took only a few quick licks. He tried to make her have more, pointing to the bowl, stirring the water with his finger and saying, "Mmmm, water, so tasty," reminding her how thirsty she'd been the day before and how sorry she was going to be later, but in the damp coolness of the morning, she wasn't interested. He gave up and drank as much as he could hold, then filled the canteen.

"Okay, Quill," he said as they started off, heading, once again, south. "Today is the day. You're going to find the birds. And I'm not going to miss."

For several hours, Erik moved carefully in Quill's wake, observing her body language. Over and over in his mind, he rehearsed what he would do when she went on point. He'd ready his gun and walk slowly forward, mentally prepared for a bird to flush at any second. When it went up, he'd wait for that moment when it seemed to hang in the air, lift his gun, sight down the barrel, and swing from behind in the direction it flew.

He was beginning to wonder if Quill's points on the previous day had been flukes, when it happened. She began sniffing intently, moving quickly down a hedgerow, her tail going faster and faster. Erik laughed, thinking she almost sounded like a snuffling pig as she snorted in huge nosefuls of scent. She worked her way to where the hedgerow ended in a field of cut grain.

In his mind's eye, Erik saw the birds moving along in front of Quill, remaining in the safety of the brush until suddenly they were forced into the open and— *ptttttttttttttrrr!* Into the air went a rooster—*blam blam blam*—and another—*blam blam*—and then four hens. And to Erik's astonishment and joy, this time one of the roosters fell!

Quill retrieved it and brought it to Erik. She sat before him, proudly holding it, and when he extended his arm she dropped it gently into his hand. It was obvious that Mike Duvochin had trained her well, but Erik refused to let himself think about that. He was struck by the simple beauty of her doing so perfectly what she had been born and bred to do. "Good girl, Quill!" he hollered. "We did it! We did it! Ya-hooo!!"

He set the bird and the gun down carefully, with the safety on. Then, unable to restrain himself, he pounced on Quill and they rolled together on the ground in a gleeful celebration. After several moments of this, Quill rose and shook herself. She spit a few stray feathers from her mouth and looked around sheepishly, as if hoping no one had witnessed this undignified display.

Then Erik picked up the bird, smoothed its feathers, and held it up to the light to admire its beauty.

The head, with its bright red mask and green and purple feathers, was magnificent. There was a perfect white ring around its neck. Depending on how the light struck them, the iridescent body feathers changed to include every color in the rainbow. The breast feathers, delicately tipped in black, shaded from rust to gold to amber, purple and blue-green. The tail feathers, well over a foot long, were striped with black and brown.

The bird's head flopped heavily to the side, and Erik was suddenly aware of the finality of what he had done. Holding the limp, warm body that had been so full of life just a moment ago, he was flooded with a powerful remorse. This bird had hatched from an egg, been raised by a mother, and survived despite brutal weather and the sharp, watching eyes of hawks and owls and coyotes. Now it was dead, and he had killed it. The enormity of this settled upon him, and the exhilaration of a moment before mixed with regret. He felt as if he, Quill, and the pheasant had each played a part in a scene as ancient and natural as the earth itself. Still, he couldn't help feeling sorrow about it, even as he was grateful for the meat and proud of his and Quill's accomplishment.

Before he put the bird in his pack, he whispered a

thank-you to it. Someday, he knew, both he and Quill would die, too. Would their bodies then nourish plants or grass that would allow a creature such as a pheasant to live? He hoped so. These thoughts were new for him, and he continued to mull them over as he and Quill walked on.

They ate the remaining cookies for their lunch. It was the last of their "civilized" food. That night, they would eat from the land.

Mindful of the need to camp near water, Erik began to look for a suitable spot. Quill's tongue was dragging again by the time they found a large pothole with cattails growing on the west edge and some scrubby bushes on the east. The water wasn't too gross-looking, at least not until Quill charged in to drink and cool herself off. That was okay, Erik thought. He could go around to the other side to get water, then boil it once he had a fire going.

A dead poplar tree that looked as if it had been hit by lightning stood bravely in the middle of the grass-land. Some of its branches littered the ground, and others were easily within Erik's reach. They were per-fect for firewood, which was good because he was starving, and eager to cook and eat his first wild bird.

Taking it from his pack, he held it up in the late

afternoon light and admired it once again. He had to clean it now, he knew that. He had to pluck it and gut it and prepare it for cooking. For a moment, he panicked. *I have no clue how to do this!* Then he told himself to relax, think, and proceed logically.

First, the tail feathers. He pulled them out, tied them with a long blade of prairie grass, and put them in his pack for a keepsake. Then, holding the bird in his left hand, he plucked handfuls of soft feathers from the breast. He was relieved to discover they were much less tenacious than the stiff tail feathers and came out fairly easily, leaving behind the wrinkled, pinky-yellow skin. He worked his way down the legs to the spurred and scaly feet, then down the back.

Quill found this very interesting and dove into the piles of feathers, coming up with several stuck to her nose, then approached to sniff the bird intently.

"If you think it smells good now, Quill, you just wait until it's cooked," Erik told her.

The bird, naked except for its feathered head and wings, didn't look quite as noble as it had before. It was also a lot smaller than he had imagined, with much less meat on it than on the chickens his mom brought home from the supermarket. It sort of reminded Erik of the scrawny rubber chicken Patrick had given him for a gag gift on his birthday. He smiled, thinking how amazed Patrick would be if he knew Erik was hunting on his own in North Dakota, with his own bird dog.

The smile quickly faded, though, when he realized it was time to get down to the *real* work of cleaning the bird. With his Swiss Army knife, he cut off the head, following with the wings and the feet.

He remembered Patrick's dad talking about checking the birds' crops to discover what they'd been eating. This would reveal the kind of habitat they'd been frequenting. He cut into the base of the throat and there it was: the "gizzard." Mr. Holt had explained that food the bird ate stayed there for a while, getting ground up by the action of the gizzard and small stones the birds ate. Then it could be more easily digested.

Inside the transparent membrane Erik could see the yellow of wheat. That made sense. He cut it open to see what else might be there, and to his surprise he found the shiny black bodies of crickets.

He wasn't sure what this information meant, exactly, in terms of finding more birds, but he thought it was very interesting. Quill seemed to think so, too.

There was no more postponing it. He took a deep

breath and sliced into the belly below the breast, exposing the guts. They were slimy and disgusting-looking, and were already stinky. He recalled Mr. Holt saying he always "field-dressed" his birds, removing the innards immediately so they didn't contaminate the meat. Next time, he would do the same. He removed the guts and carried them off into the grass a ways.

Quill followed at his heels. "No," he told her. "Wait for the meat."

Then he rinsed the bird as well as he could in the pothole. It was time to get the fire going. He searched the brush until he found two fairly large rocks and placed them about six inches apart. Then he piled some dried grass between them and put sticks over the grass. The mess kit pot he set over the wood, edges perched on the rocks. Perfect. He filled the pot with water from the side of the pothole neither he nor Quill had disturbed, set it back on the rocks, and lit the fire.

While he waited for the water to boil, he found a fairly stout stick, sharpened the end, and skewered the bird with it. He placed the bird over the fire, to the side of the pot.

Erik had been so intent on his preparations that he hadn't noticed that Quill had disappeared. He called her, and she returned quickly, looking guilty and licking her chops. "Yuck, Quill," said Erik. "You ate those guts, didn't you?"

She sat, gazing off into the distance, the picture of innocence, and Erik laughed. "I guess a pioneer dog would have done the same thing, huh, girl?" he said. "Nothing gets wasted, right? Well, they're all yours. You don't have to feel guilty about not sharing."

The sun was sinking fast, and Erik was glad he'd started early to make camp. The unfamiliar task of cleaning the bird had taken much longer than he'd realized. He set out the plastic bag for his ground cloth, unrolled his sleeping bag, and got organized while there was still light to see by. Then he and Quill sat by the fire, waiting for the water to boil and the bird to roast.

He had been hungry and thirsty before, but never anything close to the way he was feeling now. His eyes were riveted on the pot of water and the bird. Nothing seemed to be happening. He wished he'd started the fire under the water earlier. When he stuck his finger in the pot, it was barely warm. *What the heck?* he wondered. *How long does it take to boil water, anyhow?* At home it would have taken just a few minutes on the stovetop or in the microwave. He added more wood to the fire and blew on it. The flames blazed higher. He put the lid on the pot; maybe that would help. After a while, the water began to steam ever so slightly, but the bird didn't seem to be cooking at all. The skin was still pale, not even close to turning a crispy brown.

The water steamed and steamed, but never came to a real boil. Afraid it would all disappear before it got fully hot, Erik took the pot off the rocks and set it in the grass to cool. He knew he had to drink some of the water tonight. People could live without food a lot longer than they could survive without water. He thought drinking enough must be especially important with all the walking he was doing in the dry prairie air.

He rearranged the bird over the fire and concentrated on it as the stars came out and his stomach growled. Quill half napped beside him. Her eyes were closed, but her nose twitched at the smell of cooking meat that was—finally!—wafting her way. Erik's own eyes felt heavy, but much more than sleep he wanted *food*. At one point, he must have nodded off, though, because he snapped awake to see that the exposed ends of the spit had burned through and the bird had fallen into the fire. He pulled it out. The skin on one side was scorched and the entire thing was covered in a fine film of ash, but it smelled wonderful.

Finally, when he could stand waiting no longer, he put the bird on the mess kit plate. It didn't look quite like the perfectly browned birds on the platter in the photo in Dan's shoebox, but to Erik's famished eyes it looked utterly delectable. He carved off half the meat and put it in Quill's bowl, but held it away from her to allow it to cool a bit.

"I know, I know," he told her. "It's hard to wait. But you don't want to burn your tongue."

And then they ate.

In his former life, Erik would have called part of the meat raw, and part of it he'd surely have told his mother was burned. He would undoubtedly have complained about the pellets in the meat from the bird shot. But now he barely noticed these things. To him, the bird tasted of the prairie. It was smoky and rich and wild. By comparison, store-bought chicken was tasteless, boring, *dull*. Wild pheasant was the finest food there was, no doubt about it!

Quill seemed to agree.

When Erik had finished the meat, he chewed and sucked on the bones before handing them to Quill to polish off. All too soon, there was nothing left. Erik licked his fingers for every last smidgen of flavor, then sat back with a sigh of contentment.

This contentment didn't last, however, as he almost immediately realized that he was still hungry. Very hungry.

He knew Quill had to be hungry, too.

Well, he'd just have to try to fill his belly with water. He examined the pot. The water looked pretty clear. There were just a few specks of something that had sunk to the bottom. Were the pioneers afraid of a little dirt? Did they have time to stop and boil their water every time they were thirsty? It seemed unlikely. What about when they were being chased by Indians?

Erik looked at Quill, who was lapping happily from the pothole. He poured water into his cup and drank deeply, again and again, then let out a loud belch. He felt he and Quill had done well.

But he knew they were going to have to do much better if they were going to make it.

16

Erik slept fitfully, visited by strange, disjointed dreams. In one his parents were being pursued by faceless bad guys in a strange land. In another, he raced about the prairie on four legs like Quill, amazed by his own speed and agility. In the last, his grandmother, frantic with worry about him, had called Mr. Poole, his elementary-school principal, to track him down. As Mr. Poole closed in on his hiding place, Erik became so anxious he felt sick—so very, very sick . . .

He awoke then, clutching his stomach. A painful cramp seized him, followed by another. He leaped to his feet and managed to walk a few steps before becoming ill. Sinking to his knees, he spewed the contents of his stomach onto the ground in a series of violent spasms. Lifting his head shakily, he felt the cramps moving lower and knew with dread that his illness was not going to be limited to vomiting.

Hours passed during which Erik was racked by fever and sickness. Finally, spent and exhausted, he lay faceup on his sleeping bag. Chills kept alternating with drenching sweats, and now he felt he was burning up. He gazed into Quill's uncomprehending face and wondered if he was dreaming again. Who was this creature who had been by his side all morning, staring at him with what had felt like concern and confusion? When he came to his senses enough to remember that this was Quill, that she was *his dog*, a stab of happiness pierced his misery.

He forced himself to sit up. He felt dizzy, hollowed out.

"Hey, Quill," he said weakly. Quill gave an excited bark and started to run, looking back as if to say, "Finally! Let's *go*!"

"Hang on a second," Erik mumbled. He knew Quill had to be hungry, and that he, too, needed food even though the idea of eating revolted him at the moment.

But his mouth—it was so dry. He tried to lick his parched lips, but nothing happened. He needed water.

Water. Was it the unboiled water that had made

him so sick? Or maybe the parts of the bird that weren't cooked all the way through? He didn't know. Watching Quill, who was merrily stalking a mouse, he envied her for being able to eat pheasant innards and drink contaminated water without so much as a burp.

Erik's shoulders sagged. He had been careless, and careless people didn't survive. He wouldn't survive, either, unless he got some food and water soon. Feeling weary, he got to his feet and started gathering wood. When he had a proper fire going, he filled the pot and waited, stoking the flames from time to time with sticks and grass, for it to bubble. He let it boil for several minutes, wishing he knew if there was some kind of rule about how long it took to kill the bugs in there. He waited some more, this time for the water to cool. As he did, he began to feel better, stronger.

A stiff breeze had come up from the northwest, bringing much colder air with it, so he put on his warmest clothing. Then he forced himself to drink the water in small, slow sips. When it was gone he boiled more to fill his canteen and, at last, he felt ready to move on.

He had recovered enough to feel his hunger return. He guessed the time to be about ten or eleven o'clock.

His pack held nothing at all to eat, and Erik had just one thought in mind: finding food.

After about an hour of walking, he noticed that Quill was moving quickly, her nose down, tail wagging. Expecting a bird to go up any minute, he was unprepared when a jackrabbit appeared and started racing across the field. Erik didn't think to shoot it until it was too far away.

Quill, who approached birds slowly in order to point and hold them, showed no such restraint when it came to the rabbit. She took off after it, giving high-pitched, excited yips that sounded to Erik like a rusty gate swinging back and forth in the wind.

He laughed at first, watching the jackrabbit dodge and weave with Quill in hot pursuit. But when Quill had run well over a mile and was out of sight, he became concerned. He followed, calling for her until he grew hoarse, fighting down the panic that rose in his chest at the idea of losing her. Mike Duvochin had said she ran off on him. Maybe it had happened just this way.

Not knowing what to do, Erik sank down in the grass. He had no chance of finding Quill. She would have to find him. If she wanted to. He couldn't bear to think what he'd do if she didn't.

Finally, he saw her, a tiny speck on the horizon moving slowly toward him. Something about her gait looked strange to him. When she approached at last, she was panting heavily. Her tongue was hanging out, her tail was drooping, and she was favoring her right front leg.

Any notion of a scolding was forgotten. Erik held her head and rubbed his face along her cheek. Then he lifted her leg and examined it carefully, pressing down the length of it from shoulder to foot, gently bending each joint.

"Oh, Quill," he said softly. "What have you done to yourself?"

He worked his way back up the leg, and she let out a little whine when he reached the joint below her shoulder. There was nothing obvious there, no cut, no bleeding, no sharp thorn. Erik figured she must have strained or torn a muscle, and hoped it wasn't too serious.

He emptied half the water from the canteen and watched as she lapped it all up. Then she lay down in the grass, tongue dripping, still panting. Erik took a small sip of water and sat beside her to wait for her to cool down.

After a while Quill got up and looked around, her

nose twitching. She looked at Erik as if to say, "I'm ready. You?" And she began trotting across the field. She limped slightly with every step, but didn't appear to take any notice of it.

Erik admired her spirit but at the same time he worried about her. What would happen if she became too lame to walk? To hunt? They would starve for sure.

He imagined how good that rabbit would have tasted and promised himself he'd be ready to shoot whatever Quill found, whether it flew, ran, climbed a tree, or slithered on the ground. He paused for a moment, wondering if he was hungry enough to eat snake. The answer was yes. Yep, he sure was. He was pretty sure he remembered somebody saying it tasted like chicken, but everyone had laughed afterwards, so he wasn't sure if it was true or not.

By late afternoon, Erik had drunk all his water and missed two roosters. In desperation, he took a shot at a hen. It came down, and Quill retrieved it. Guiltily, Erik field-dressed it and put it into his pack.

It was time to start looking for a place to stop for the night. Quill's leg seemed to have recovered, but he didn't want to push her any farther than he had to.

Ahead, Erik could see some buildings. The temptation of finding easy water from a spigot, as he had before, drew him closer. He leashed Quill and they sneaked forward a few steps at a time, taking cover where they could, ready to drop to the ground at the first sign of a person.

There was a farmhouse at the end of a long driveway, but it had a deserted look about it. The roof was caved in on one side and the porch was falling off. As they drew closer, he saw that several of the windows were broken. There were two cars up on blocks and a rusty truck with the hood raised. Erik had the feeling it had been that way for a long time.

All the left-behind, empty houses he'd seen in town had depressed him, but now he was grateful for the way people out here seemed to just up and go, leaving a house to fall slowly to ruin. He couldn't help wondering what made them do it, and what had brought them out here in the first place.

From behind a poplar tree, he got a good look at the yard. There was a barn, an empty corn crib, and a smaller building that could have been a shed or a workshop.

He peeked in the barn and then in the shed, and saw no sign of people, or of a source of water. He was about to turn away when his eye caught on something sitting on top of the workbench. It was the familiar, brightly colored wrapper of a bag of Doritos. Mesmerized by the sight, Erik opened the door and went inside, telling himself not to get his hopes up, that the bag was surely empty. But it was full, and unopened. And beside it, in a litter of used paper coffee cups and crumpled wrappers, was a small bag of peanuts and a Snickers bar. Next to that were two cans of Mountain Dew, still attached to the plastic rings that had once held a six-pack.

The packages containing the food had been nibbled on, probably by mice. The soda cans were covered in a fine layer of dust. All of it sat on the workbench trapped amid a tangle of old spiderwebs and dead flies.

It was *beautiful*.

Erik stared at this unexpected bounty, his mouth watering as he imagined the salty taste of the peanuts and chips, followed by the sweetness of the candy. He grabbed the chips bag and held it up so Quill, who was sniffing around in the corner, could see it. Then he ripped it open, stuffed a handful into his mouth, and held out another handful for Quill.

The flood of flavor in his mouth was delicious. He continued eating, one handful for him, one for Quill, followed by a sip of soda, until the bag was empty. The peanuts he shared with Quill, but not the candy bar.

As he unhooked her leash, he explained to her that he wasn't being selfish, it was just that he remembered Patrick and Mr. Holt talking about the time Hot Spots ate an entire chocolate cake and nearly died. Erik didn't know if the coating on a candy bar was enough chocolate to make a dog sick, but he wasn't taking any chances.

Besides, he told her, several times during the day he had noticed her chewing on things she had come across in her travels: grass, bones, dead animals, and, he suspected, rabbit poop. He comforted himself with the thought that she had a lot more in her stomach than he did.

As they trudged on, Erik realized that he had just helped himself to someone else's property without thinking twice about it. Earlier in the day, he'd shot a hen pheasant, something no respectable hunter would do. In the space of a single afternoon, it seemed, he'd embarked on a career in crime, going from being a mere Liar and Runaway to Poacher, Trespasser, and now Thief.

A small voice inside reminded him that he had become a thief when he ran off with Quill. She didn't really belong to him, even if her owner didn't deserve her.

Doubts about what he was doing crowded his thoughts. Was he really living off the land if he was eating Doritos and slugging down Mountain Dew? Did the fact that he was trying to survive make it okay to do things he knew were wrong? These thoughts made him uncomfortable, and he tried to put them out of his mind.

When he saw the straight line of a road about a quarter mile ahead, he put his hand on Quill's collar to control her. They approached slowly and carefully. A car appeared in the far distance, a plume of dust following in its path. They hid in some brush to wait for it to pass. Erik hunkered down as low as he could, pulling Quill down with him. Peering through the leaves of the bush that concealed them, he saw that the vehicle was a sheriff's patrol car, traveling very slowly. Was the driver on the lookout for a lost kid and a dog? Erik's heart started beating fast. They were well hidden, weren't they? To his relief, the car continued to creep down the road and finally disappeared from sight.

He wondered if it really had been looking for him and, if so, how many others were searching. There was no way to know. He and Quill had been careful, but they were going to have to be extra vigilant from here on out.

About an hour later, he staggered over a rise to see Quill wading chest deep in a pothole, slurping away, oblivious to the mud her feet stirred up. Quickly, Erik ran to the far side where the water was undisturbed and held the pot under the surface. As it filled, he thought about the eternity it would take to make a fire, get the water to boil, and wait for it to cool down afterwards.

They were well out of sight of any roads. This was a good place to camp. He cleaned the hen pheasant, surprised by how much smaller it was than a male, then made a fire and started the bird roasting and the water simmering.

The wind started to blow much more strongly, in sudden gusts that caused the smoke from the fire to swirl unpredictably. Erik's eyes were stinging and it was dark by the time the bird was cooked. He tried to eat slowly, to savor the rich flavor, but the meat was soon gone and, once again, he was left feeling hungry.

As Quill crunched the bones, Erik lay on his back and listened and watched. The wind blew even harder, bringing in clouds that obscured the stars. It howled and roared, louder than the noises of the night animals and sounding at times like a wild creature itself.

Erik got up and put on his warm jacket, then snuggled into his sleeping bag beside Quill, feeling proud. Despite everything, they had made it for three whole days.

17

Something was tickling Erik's nose. Without opening his eyes or fully wakening, he brushed his hand across his face. Another tickle. With a groan, he rolled over and pulled the sleeping bag up over his head. Something wet and cold ran along the side of his cheek and into his ear.

He sat up abruptly, and was astounded to see that it was snowing! His mom had been right: the weather in North Dakota could change mighty fast. Yesterday he'd been wearing a T-shirt.

Ordinarily, Erik loved snow and everything about it: days off from school, building snow forts, going sledding and snowboarding. He didn't even mind shoveling snow most of the time. But it quickly dawned on him that in his present circumstances snow could be a real problem. Quill, who was curled up in a tight ball, seemed to know it, too. She shivered, barely lifting her head.

With mixed feelings of awe and dread, he took in the scene around him. The snowflakes were not falling softly and silently like in a snow globe or a Christmas special on TV. They were being driven almost sideways by the fierce north wind that blew across the open prairie land, only landing when there was an obstacle on the ground to stop them. Like his body. Erik noticed that a drift of snow had built up on the side of his sleeping bag.

A snowstorm was fun to be out in if you had a warm house to return to, where a cup of hot chocolate waited. But he and Quill had none of that. They needed to find some shelter.

Ignoring the complaints from his empty stomach, he reluctantly climbed out of his sleeping bag and put on his warm clothing and rain jacket, glad that he had chosen a dark green color when he'd picked it out at the mall. He knew that staying dry was important. His sleeping bag was damp on the side, but not too bad. He rolled it up, tied it to his pack, and covered the pack the best he could with one of the large plastic bags he'd brought.

Shouldering his gun, he called to Quill. To his relief, she showed no sign of limping. They started off with the wind at their backs. Still, it seemed to cut right through his clothes, and the wet cold stung his exposed face and hands. He hoped moving would help to warm him and Quill, too, until he could find a sheltered place to build a fire.

After a short time they reached a dry pothole with a ring of knee-high brush around the edge. The blowing snow had caught on the brush and drifted here, too. To Erik's surprise, Quill immediately grew birdy and froze almost instantly on a hard point.

All Erik's concerns about the snow and cold vanished. He raised his gun and got ready, then moved forward with slow careful steps, crooning in a low, calm voice, "Whoa, Quill, good girl. What have we got here, huh?"

Quill held to a solid point until Erik was close enough to reach down and touch her. Still no bird went up. He walked past her in the direction she was pointing and stomped down hard with one foot, then another. A rooster pheasant exploded up out of a powdery snowdrift, cackling noisily. Erik took aim, waited to let the bird get far enough away so that his shot—if it hit—wouldn't tear the meat up too badly. Instead of the panicked rush he'd experienced with his first couple of birds, everything now seemed to unfold in slow motion. First Quill's point. Then the flush of the bird. Lift the gun. Swing. Now. Shoot.

The rooster tumbled from the sky. Quill started over to retrieve it, but turned in mid-stride to lock into another focused point only a few yards from where Erik stood. It seemed impossible that another bird would be holding so close by, what with Erik stomping around, the rooster going up, and Erik shooting. But Erik wasn't going to make the mistake of doubting Quill again. He wondered if it was something about the snow that was making the birds sit tight rather than fly or run.

Sure enough, when Erik approached the spot Quill was pointing, another rooster went up. Again, Erik saw everything happen with a slow, eerie clarity as he carefully swung, shot, and watched the bird fall from the sky.

Again, Quill started off to retrieve it and, caught by the scent of another bird, went on point. This time, Erik saw several birds scurrying every which way through the brush. Quill broke her point and began chasing them, her tail beating back and forth a mile a minute. Then, one right after another, they all broke from the cover and took to the air.

Erik told himself not to be distracted by the wild flurry rising all about him. Instead, he picked out one rooster and focused on it, willing his mind to *slow down, see, swing, shoot.* The bird dropped.

In a frenzy of excitement, Quill raced after the fallen birds. She picked up one, then dropped it to grab another, then dropped that to return to the first. Erik laughed, watching her race from one bird to another, unable to decide which to pick up. Finally she paused, and Erik thought it was almost as if she was telling herself to settle down and make a plan. Then, methodically, she picked up one bird, brought it to Erik, went for the second, brought it back, and went for the third.

When Erik had all three birds in hand, he set them on the ground and dropped to his knees. Throwing his arms around Quill's neck, he shouted gleefully, "We're gonna eat like kings today! You are the most amazing, incredible, wild, crazy, bird-dogginest bird dog in the entire world!"

Quill looked away modestly for a moment. Then she lifted her head and let out a long "Aaaroooo," and

Erik threw caution to the wind and howled along with her. Grinning to himself, Erik reflected that another nice thing about the prairie was that you could act like a total lunatic and there was no one around to see or hear. Recovering himself, he field-dressed the birds and put them in his pack.

It was still snowing. Now that they had solved their food problem, Erik realized he was wet and getting cold. He thought that, even though it was early, he should begin looking for a place where he and Quill could shelter themselves for the night. After an hour or so, a dilapidated barn came into view. When he had checked it out from a distance, he and Quill went closer. There were no footprints, no car tracks, no signs of people. Erik was also happy to see there was enough snow drifted along the southeast wall to solve the problem of finding water. Peeking into the barn, he felt a sense of elation. It was deserted. There were some bales of straw stacked against one wall. The straw would come in handy for starting a fire and, when it was spread out, would make a soft bed as well.

His feet were freezing. He took off his pack, left it inside the barn, and went out to scout around for firewood. A jackrabbit ran out of the brush pile he was scavenging in, and he was glad he had kept his gun with him. He couldn't believe it when his shot was true. Quill retrieved the rabbit but, unlike with the birds, which she always brought right to Erik's waiting hand, she didn't seem to know what to do with it. Finally, she dropped it about twenty feet from Erik and ran off to sniff around the base of a tree in a show of disinterest.

Erik laughed. "So you only like to chase rabbits, not retrieve them, is that right?" he asked. "Well, I bet you won't have any trouble eating one!"

He cleaned the three birds and the rabbit, pleasantly surprised by how easily the rabbit's fur coat slipped off, then built his fire right on the dirt floor of the barn. The wood he'd gathered burned cleanly enough that the wind, beating against the cracks and gaps in the barn walls, made for adequate ventilation. He put a pot of snow over the fire to melt.

As it grew dark, the wind continued its inhuman howling. Erik didn't mind the wind. Sheltered from it and from the snow, he felt quite cozy in the circle of firelight and warmth he shared with Quill.

He was beginning to get the hang of cooking meat on an open fire. The birds and the rabbit were evenly roasted, or at least pretty evenly. And the meat tasted wonderful. After the meal, stomach full at last, he lay on his side watching the fire.

The trouble was, now that he was free to concentrate on something besides his hunger, his mind began to fill with all the depressing thoughts that he'd been trying to avoid. Surely Oma had called his parents. They had to be furious with him, as well as frantic with worry.

Had Oma also called the police? Probably. Uneasily, he recalled all the stories about missing children he'd heard on TV. Some of them became big news. Was his picture—the dorky one where his ears looked enormous—plastered all over the nightly news?

For the first time, he asked himself what it was that he was really doing. Living a wild life, he had told himself. But now he had to admit that was only true up to a point. In so many ways, he was glad he'd had these days on the prairie with Quill. He would never forget them. But what was his Big Plan? To *head south*. Until what? He reached Mexico? Argentina? To *live off the land*. Brilliant. Eating birds and stolen junk food? For how long, forever? Until he was eighteen?

These dismal thoughts were interrupted by a muffled noise from outside the barn. It sounded like the slam of a car door. Quill heard it, too, and let out two sharp barks before Erik managed to shush her.

Panicked, Erik jumped up but quickly realized that

he and Quill had nowhere to go. He'd been so happy to take shelter in the barn that he hadn't thought about how it would act as a trap if anyone came upon them.

Straining, Erik could hear footsteps, followed by the creak of the barn door swinging open and the increased volume of the wind, which continued to gust violently. The beam of a flashlight swept the dimness of the barn, landed on the fire, which flared and burned brighter from the air blowing in from the doorway, and then on Erik's feet. The light rose to his knees and then his face, and stayed there, blinding him. He staggered out of the way of it, but it followed him.

The door closed, lessening the wind's howl. In the relative quiet, a man's voice said, "I know who you are. I saw you on TV. A kid and a dog like this one, both gone missing. There's a reward for bringin' you back, and I guess I'll be the one to claim it."

18

Erik stood blinking in the glare of the flashlight beam, too astounded to respond. Quill remained by his side, growling low in her throat.

"Seems it's my lucky day," the man went on, sounding both pleased and amused. "Buddy asks me to come out this way, check on some horses. So I'm heading back and I see a light and what looks like smoke coming from this old barn. I'm thinking to myself, *That just isn't right.* So I come in here and what do you know?" The man gave a snort of laughter. "Thanks, kid. I sure can use the five thousand bucks."

Erik hadn't moved except to put his hands up to shield his eyes. From behind his hands he said, "Five thousand bucks?"

The man lowered the flashlight and said, "Yeah.

So put out that fire and grab your stuff. Time to stop playing Davy Crockett and get on home to your momma." In a more kindly tone he added, "I bet you could use a home-cooked meal by now, couldn't you, son?"

Erik said tightly, "I'm not your son, and my mother is in Iraq."

The man smiled. "Oh, yeah, I remember now. It was your grandma on the TV, the one who put up the money, wasn't it? You know they got one of those Amber Alerts out on you?"

An image of Oma, weeping on TV and begging for Erik's safe return, flashed through his head.

"The old man—that your grandpa? He was plenty upset."

Yeah, I bet, thought Erik, imagining Big Darrell's fury.

The man waved the flashlight around, saying, "Come on, now, you've caused enough trouble. Put that fire out and let's get going."

Thoughts were racing through Erik's mind like tumbleweeds across the prairie. Five thousand dollars? Oma and Big Darrell didn't have that kind of money. Look at their house. They couldn't even afford to fix the porch steps. There was no way he was going to let himself be hauled back by this stranger and make his grandparents pay to get him back. It was too late to fix the fact that he'd run away, but he could sure as heck decide how and when he was going back. And he was going to do it on his own, not be handed over like a lost wallet.

He figured his best chance of escape was to pretend to give up and surrender to the idea that he was being taken back home. With a shrug, he mumbled, "Okay," and used a stick to spread the remains of fire. Then he stamped the embers out and began gathering his belongings, starting with the shotgun.

Before Erik knew what was happening, the man reached out and grabbed the gun from his hand. Grinning, he said, "I'll hang on to this for now, if you don't mind. I don't want you getting any funny ideas."

"Hey! You can't take that! It belonged to my uncle," Erik cried. At the sound of his raised voice, Quill began to bark.

"Quiet!" the man commanded her. To Erik, he said, "Keep your pants on, kid. You'll get the gun back once I've got you home and the money's in my pocket."

"Don't worry, I'm not going to get any 'funny' ideas," Erik said, making himself sound meek and resigned. "I'm ready to go back now."

The man nodded approvingly as Erik picked up his pack. "That's the way, kid."

They walked in the light of the flashlight beam toward the barn door. Every one of Erik's senses was on full alert, waiting for just the right moment to make a move. The man pushed the door open into what felt like a different world from the warm, cozy barn. It was pitch-dark. Snow was still falling, driven sideways by the screaming wind.

The flashlight beam landed on a pickup truck about twenty yards away. Erik was pleased to see that the man had driven right up to the barn wall and parked, meaning that he'd have to back up before he could come after Erik, giving Erik a couple of extra precious seconds to get away.

"Go on, you and the dog, get in the front seat," the man hollered.

"Okay," Erik yelled back. When they got near the truck, he opened the passenger side door as if to get in, but as the man walked around the rear of the truck to the driver's side, Erik took off. Quill followed, barking with excitement.

As Erik fled into the blowing snow and darkness, he heard the man shouting angrily, but the words were snatched away by the wind. Then the flashlight beam swept wildly through the night. It caught Erik's back for a brief moment, but he dodged to the side and was soon beyond its range.

As he stumbled blindly on, he envied Quill, who seemed to have no trouble at all navigating obstacles and uneven ground in the black of night. Erik remembered his dream of—when was it, two nights before?—in which he, too, had run smoothly and effortlessly on four legs.

He looked back to see that the truck was moving, its headlights cutting a swath of light through the darkness. They moved in an arc as the man drove in a circle. But the truck couldn't follow through brush and rocks, fences and ditches. When Erik dared to slow down enough to look back, he was elated to see the lights of the pickup fading in the distance. He paused, bending double to catch his breath, then allowed himself a small smile of satisfaction. They had escaped!

19

When Erik finally paused to rest, he tried to reason out what the man might do next. With no kid to present for a reward, would he just go home and forget the whole thing? Or would he tell the police where he'd seen Erik, figuring the information might be worth something? Might he try to get some money from Oma and Big Darrell for Uncle Dan's gun? The possibilities ran circles through his head until he gave up trying to guess. All he could do, he figured, was decide on a plan of his own.

To his relief, he realized that the storm appeared to have blown itself out. The cold front that had swooped in so ferociously, bringing the snow with it, had passed. One by one, stars began to show themselves, and a three-quarter moon became visible. After a while, Erik was able to spot the Big Dipper and, from there, to find the North Star.

He'd been running south. Now he would follow the star and head north. He reached down and hugged Quill to him, hard. Then he stood up and started walking.

Using the stars, they walked through the night, and when the sun rose they kept on, moving steadily north. When Erik was thirsty he ate snow, and Quill did the same. Quill's energy never flagged in the clear, cool air, though Erik felt his own pace slow from time to time. With no gun and no food, they didn't stop to hunt or eat or sleep.

Quill scrounged food wherever she could: dead mice and moles, scat from various animals, things Erik couldn't identify and wasn't sure he wanted to. Oddly, he didn't feel hungry. A vague but strong sense of purpose gripped him, driving him to retrace his steps back to where he had started.

As he walked, it seemed to him he was seeing the life of the prairie with great sharpness and clarity. He stopped to watch a coyote hunting in the grass for mice, pouncing, chasing, pouncing and chasing like a kitten at play. When the coyote finally looked up and saw him, it went slinking away. He watched a marsh hawk soar low along the ground and dip gracefully to catch a mouse in its talons, and saw a red-tailed hawk drop from the bare branches of a lightning-scarred tree to snag a pheasant from the grass below. When they came to a wide area of rolling hillocks, they spooked a covey of sharp-tailed grouse. Erik heard, for the first time, their alarm call, *Ooo-ooo-ooo, ooo-ooo-ooo*, as they flew over the next rise and disappeared.

Night fell again and still they kept on. Erik's eyes became accustomed to the darkness, and he was aided by the light from the moon and the flames of one of the gas fires burning at an oil rig on the outskirts of Fortuna. When he recognized the barn and corral where he had gotten water his first night out, he felt proud that he was on the right track, that he was finding his way.

And then, several hours later, he came to the straight line of trees bordering the side of his grandparents' farmhouse. He approached, and the house itself loomed before him. When he walked around the corner and stood for a moment at the porch steps, he saw a bluish light coming from the downstairs window. Creeping closer, he peered in and saw Big

Darrell sitting and watching the snowy picture on the old television set.

The sight of his grandfather caused him to stop, his heart thudding nervously. He watched for several moments, wondering what Big Darrell, who kept farmer's hours, was doing up at what had to be close to two o'clock in the morning. Probably he was too angry to sleep, and was contemplating what he'd do when he got his hands on Erik at last.

Quill, perhaps anxious either to go inside or move on, let out a little whine, and Big Darrell, startled, lifted his head to listen. He stood, walked to the door, and opened it, gazing blindly into the darkness for a moment. "Dan?" he called in a low voice. "Dan?" Then he shook his head and rubbed his eyes and peered closely at Erik, who must have appeared to him as nothing more than a shadowy shape. "Erik, is that you?"

"Yes," Erik said, climbing up the stairs, mindful of the broken step Oma had warned him about the first night he'd come. It seemed a very long time ago. "It's me."

He reached the porch, Quill following, and stopped, facing his grandfather. Before he could say anything more, Big Darrell gathered him in a clumsy embrace, made more awkward by the pack on Erik's back.

In the silence afterwards, Big Darrell said in a voice so low Erik had to strain to hear, "I lost one boy. Didn't think I could stand to lose another."

20

Erik was too stunned to speak. To his relief, he was saved from answering by Big Darrell, who cleared his throat and said hoarsely, "I expect you could use some food."

"Aren't you going to yell at me?" Erik asked. He was sure that's what his parents would have done, once they'd seen that he was safely home. It was certainly what he'd expected from Big Darrell.

"I'll leave that to your grandma," Big Darrell said with a tired smile.

In the porch light, Erik saw the weariness etched into Big Darrell's face, and understood for the first time how much both of his grandparents must have suffered while he was gone. "I-I'm sorry, Big Darrell. Was Oma real upset?"

"I'd guess she lost two pounds for every day you were gone."

Erik winced. "What about my parents?"

"We were going to tell them in the morning."

"You didn't tell them yet?" Erik asked incredulously.

Big Darrell shrugged. "There didn't seem any point to it, not until we knew something for sure. There was nothing they could do, all the way over there, and your grandma didn't want to upset them. She kept saying—hoping, really—that you'd come back."

Erik shook his head in wonder. He was relieved that he wasn't in big trouble—with his parents, anyway—and deeply puzzled by the apparent change in his grandfather.

He started to follow Big Darrell inside, then paused, looking down at Quill, who was sitting and waiting patiently. "What about—" he began.

Before he could finish, Big Darrell surprised him again by saying, "The dog, too. I don't need to ask if *she's* hungry, not if she's like Elvis was."

Sitting in a chair in the warm kitchen seemed unreal to Erik after his days and nights outdoors. To add to the unreality, Big Darrell was acting—nice. He had allowed Quill into the house without blinking an eye. He and Erik were having a normal sort of conversation. After so much time spent talking to no one but Quill, all of this was making Erik feel a little punchy. "Oh, she's hungry, all right," he said. "You got any dead moles? Rabbit poop?"

Big Darrell laughed, a deep hearty sound Erik hadn't heard before. Then he glanced toward the ceiling and said, "I hope I didn't wake your grandmother. I think she might finally be getting some sleep."

They didn't say anything for a while, as Big Darrell moved from the counter to the stovetop to the toaster, his brow knit with concentration. Watching him, Erik guessed that Oma did almost all the cooking and that the kitchen was unfamiliar territory for his grandfather. But Big Darrell worked carefully and methodically, and the mouthwatering smells of sizzling butter and frying eggs and ham soon filled the room.

The quiet felt comfortable, not at all like the charged and hostile silence that had surrounded Big Darrell before. Erik was glad for the change, even if he didn't understand it, and he was so tired he almost dozed off sitting at the little oak table. When the food was ready, Big Darrell filled two plates, slid one onto the floor for Quill and placed the other in front of Erik, along with a glass of milk.

Quill gulped her food, and so did Erik. When he'd finished with a large swig of milk, Big Darrell said, "I need to tell the sheriff's office you're back."

He made the call, saying that Erik was back, unharmed, and thanking them for their trouble.

After he hung up, he said, "The dispatcher says he can't believe nobody found you sooner. There have been a lot of folks looking, you know. We weren't sure whether you'd run off or gotten lost. The sheriff asked if maybe you got in a car with somebody and headed back to New York. We just didn't know what to think."

"I'm sorry. I thought—well, I don't know what I thought. I didn't have much of a plan. I just—"

"—wanted to get away."

Erik nodded.

"The day you took off, I came home to find the house empty. Do you know your grandmother actually got in the truck and drove off to look for you?"

"She did?" Erik asked in amazement. "But she doesn't drive . . ."

"Not for thirty-four years, she didn't. I guess she does now." Big Darrell actually grinned as he said this, and Erik grinned back.

"She's the one who figured you didn't want to be

found. She believed you'd come back when you were ready, and I guess she was right." Big Darrell was quiet for a moment. Then he let out a huge yawn and said tiredly, "I think we'd both better hit the sack."

That sounded like a wonderful idea to Erik. But before he slept, there was something he needed to confess. Big Darrell didn't seem angry, but he didn't know everything Erik had done. "A man found me and wanted to turn me in for a reward," he blurted.

Big Darrell nodded. "We got a call about that."

"I got away from him, but he—he took Dan's gun."

"We heard that, too. Seems the fellow showed up at the sheriff's office, thinking he'd get a reward for returning it. They set him straight about that. We'll be getting the gun back."

Erik let out a sigh of relief.

Big Darrell was headed for the stairs. "We can talk about all that tomorrow," he said over his shoulder. "You're home safe, that's the main thing."

Erik and Quill followed, and Big Darrell paused outside the bedroom on the left at the top of the stairs, the one that had belonged to Dan. The door was open. "Good night," he said.

Erik stood still, unsure what to do.

Big Darrell added, "It's a boy's room. Your grandmother says you should have it."

"You're sure?"

Big Darrell nodded.

Erik stood in the doorway for a moment before going into Dan's room. He was very tired, and when he looked around, he wondered if he might already be asleep and dreaming. The photograph of Dan that had been on the dresser was gone, along with the Purple Heart and the dog tags. On the wall instead of the flag was an old painting of a hunting scene.

He climbed into bed with Quill curled up beside him. He didn't know how long he'd slept when he was awakened, not by a sound, but by the peculiar sensation of being watched. He opened his eyes to see the outline of a figure standing by his bed.

"Oh, Erik!" Oma whispered. "I didn't mean to wake you. I had to see for myself, here you are! Safe and sound and—"

Her voice broke then, and Erik could hear that she had begun to cry. He got out of bed and hugged her, patting her back the way he remembered his mother doing when he was little. He felt awkward doing this, but the darkness helped. He was surprised by how glad he was to see her.

"Oma," he said in a small voice. "I'm really, really sorry."

He felt a shudder pass through her small body, which felt even more frail and birdlike to him than before, and he was filled with remorse. "I guess I wasn't thinking about—anything—or anybody—but myself."

After several moments, Oma took a deep breath and pulled away from his embrace. There was enough light so he could see her looking into his eyes. "You had your reasons for running off, I expect. Did you find some answers?"

Erik was surprised again by her question. He nodded.

"The Lord works in mysterious ways, Erik. I hope I never again have to go through anything like the last five days. But something wonderful has happened, and it couldn't have happened without you running off the way you did."

Erik shook his head, confused. "I don't know what you mean."

"You running off—it changed Big Darrell."

Erik pondered this. "He *did* seem different. Nicer. Not so scary."

"Not so *scared*," Oma corrected.

"Big Darrell, scared?" Erik scoffed. "Of what?"

Oma hesitated, seeming to wonder how to begin, or perhaps if she should begin at all. "I don't know, Erik, maybe you're too young to understand this . . ."

"I'm not."

Oma nodded thoughtfully. "No, I expect you aren't. Well, now that I've gone and woken you up . . ." She sat on the side of the bed and patted the mattress next to her. Erik sat, and Quill joined him. "You see, Erik, when we lost Dan, it—it's an awful thing to say, but at first I didn't think I wanted to live anymore. I had your mother to think about, though, and my church and my friends to help me, and slowly I learned to cope." She paused, then said sadly, "But Big Darrell wouldn't let anybody help him. He closed himself off from everyone, even your mother and me. I've tried hard to understand it, and what I think is that he was"—she hesitated—"protecting himself. Trying to make sure he'd never be hurt like that again. Do you see? If you don't love anything, you can't feel the pain of losing it." Oma sighed, then murmured, "That's the problem with grieving. The dead can begin to matter more than the living."

She touched Erik's shoulder and smiled. "Your momma couldn't stand to be around Big Darrell, the way he was so quiet and angry-acting all the time. She left as soon as she could, and it was like we lost her, too. When she sent you out here to us, I can't tell you what it meant to me. Having a boy around the house, and a dog—it brought a lot of old feelings back. Then when you left"—she shook her head—"I couldn't bring myself to tell your momma. I didn't want to worry her when there wasn't anything she could do. But also I—I couldn't bear to have her think we drove you away, too." She sighed. "And for Big Darrell, it was as if he was losing Dan all over again."

Erik recalled the man who'd caught him in the barn saying that "the old man was plenty upset." At the time, Erik had been sure that meant Big Darrell was angry. He shook his head and said again, "I'm really sorry."

"Well, I'm not," Oma said firmly.

"But—it was awful, for both of you."

"It was," Oma said, patting his hand. "But it was wonderful, too. It brought Big Darrell back."

Oma gave his hand a squeeze and got up, saying she wanted Erik to get lots of sleep, and he was left to contemplate what she had said. Every bit of it felt confusing.

He had expected to be punished, even felt he deserved to be punished. And yet, for reasons of their own, Oma and Big Darrell had forgiven him.

At the same time he felt remorse for putting his grandparents through such worry, he treasured the days he had spent on the prairie with Quill. He didn't regret any of what he'd experienced, even the bad and scary parts. He even felt a weird sort of pride that he'd been wily enough not to be found by the searchers, and that he'd come back on his own.

He had wanted to make big, real decisions that had consequences and, out alone on the prairie with Quill, he had. They had survived, and that felt good and important. But what he did mattered here, too, in the world of people and family. And he had never imagined that such a momentous change as the one that had taken place in Big Darrell could have come about because of something *he* did.

He thought of the question posed in his mother's drawing of the geese: *How will you live your own wild life?* It was a good question, after all, even for a kid. But it was one he'd have to keep asking—and answering.

There was one part of it all that he did understand clearly, the part about being afraid to lose what you love. Because he loved Quill, and now he had to give her up, and he didn't know how he was going to bear it.

21

In the morning Erik heard the phone ring. When he went downstairs, Quill scrambling behind him, he found Oma and Big Darrell sitting at the kitchen table, their expressions grim. They both smiled when they saw him, but the smiles quickly faded. They exchanged a glance and Oma said, "We'd best tell him."

Big Darrell nodded. He looked at Erik and said, "That was Mike Duvochin. He's taking the day off to come for the dog. He'll be here in about two hours."

Erik had known in his heart that this was coming. After waking, he had lain in bed steeling himself for the time when Quill's owner would come for her. And still the news struck him with such devastating force that it took his breath away. He realized part of him had held out hope that it wouldn't turn out this way, and that he and Quill would remain together.

"I'm sorry, Erik," Oma murmured into the silence of the kitchen.

Erik couldn't speak. His eyes filled with tears, and to hide them he quickly bent down to pet Quill.

Several moments passed before Oma handed him an envelope, saying gently, "This came while you were gone."

It was a letter from his parents, mailed just before they left home. His father wrote that he was proud to be serving his country, despite the upset to their lives. He said, "I hope in time you will come to understand that sometimes in life we have to do things we don't want to do. The right thing to do is sometimes the hard thing." His mother wrote that she hoped he was getting on well with Oma and was learning to stay out of Big Darrell's way, and that he didn't mind being in North Dakota too awfully much. They both said how much they loved him and looked forward to seeing him again.

Reading it, Erik marveled at how much had happened since he'd said an angry goodbye to his parents in New York. The letter in his hand might have been written to a different boy. As Oma made breakfast of bacon and pancakes, he wrote a letter back. He didn't tell about running away. There was no need to get them all riled up, especially now that he was home safely. Instead, he told about how he'd gone hunting, after all, and how great it had been, and how North Dakota was pretty cool once you got to know it. He signed it "Love, Erik," and hoped it would set their minds at ease.

After breakfast, he went outside with Quill. They walked over to the row of trees and sat, their backs to the house, facing the prairie. The weather had turned mild again, and the sun gleamed on the fields of un-harvested wheat and sunflowers as if on a golden sea.

He explained to Quill that her owner was coming for her, although he knew she didn't understand. By saying it out loud and going over and over it in his mind, he knew he was really trying to prepare himself.

"You are the best dog in the whole world, you know that, don't you? You saved my life out there. You taught me how to hunt. I'll never, ever forget you."

He wrapped his arms around her warm body and sniffed deeply so he would never forget, either, the familiar, earthy smell of her fur, which held within it the sharp, clean scent of prairie grass and open air.

He thought about losing what you love.

"What am I going to do?" he whispered into her neck.

All he could come up with was that he'd have to hold tight to his memories of their days together, and to the things he still had. He'd go to school on Monday, and maybe it wouldn't be as bad as he had feared. He'd keep on going, what else was there to do? He would do the next thing that needed doing, and the next. And try to find new things to love.

When Mike Duvochin's truck pulled into the driveway a few minutes after ten, Erik was ready. He stood up and watched as Mike got out of the cab, looked around, and spotted them.

"Hey there, Flash!" Duvochin called.

Quill ran to him, her tail wagging. Erik had prepared himself for this moment, but still it wrenched his heart. Duvochin bent down to pat her and when they had finished their greeting, he stood up.

Quill—Erik would always think of her as Quill—stood midway between them, her mouth hanging open in a dopey grin.

"You must be Erik."

Erik stepped forward and put out his hand. "Erik Carlson, sir."

Duvochin hesitated, then shook Erik's proffered hand.

Behind him, Erik heard the kitchen door open and close, and saw that Oma and Big Darrell had come out onto the porch.

Mike Duvochin nodded to them, then turned his gaze back to Erik. "Well, Erik, I don't know quite what to say to you. You stole my dog. I was mad as hell. I was considering taking legal action against you. But I hear she was in pretty bad shape from that porcupine, and you helped to doctor her."

Erik swallowed, but found he couldn't speak.

"I understand you got pretty attached to her, too."

Erik nodded.

"I can see how that would happen. She's a great dog, maybe the best I've ever had. Did she hunt for you?"

Erik nodded again, afraid to even try to talk.

"I spent a lot of hours working with her, you know. She's got all the right instincts, but a dog like this needs a lot of training to be the best she can be."

Erik managed to murmur, "I know. And she is. The best."

Duvochin shifted uncomfortably from one foot to the other and said, "Hell, I just want you to understand this dog is special."

"I know."

"If she was just any old dog, I might have let her go, but—"

"I wouldn't give her up if she was mine, either," Erik said.

Duvochin took a deep breath. "Well, listen, you probably saved her life and I'm grateful to you for that."

Erik nodded.

"Okay, then," Duvochin said, obviously uneasy and ready to be on his way, "I guess we'll be taking off . . ."

Quill was sniffing the edges of Oma's garden, and Erik called her over to say goodbye. He thanked her for being his dog for as long as she could. He whispered that he loved her. She licked his face.

Then Duvochin got into his truck and called, "Flash, here!" and she hopped right into the cab and sat beside him in the passenger seat. Erik remembered Dr. Bob saying, "That's the beauty of dogs. They don't dwell on the past." He was glad for Quill's sake that her heart wasn't being broken the way his was.

He watched until the truck disappeared. He kept on watching until the only sign of it that remained was the whirl of dust it had raised on the gravel road. When that, too, was gone, blown off by the constant prairie wind, Erik turned away. Carefully, he climbed the porch stairs to where Oma and Big Darrell stood waiting for him.

Oma placed her hand gently on his cheek for a moment, but nobody spoke. After a while, Erik took a deep breath and looked around. The broken step caught his eye. He pointed to it and said to Big Darrell, "I saw some tools and scraps of lumber in the barn. If you want, we could try to fix that busted step today."

Big Darrell gazed down at the porch as if he were seeing it for the first time in a long time. Then he looked at Erik and nodded. "All right," he said.

Oma beamed at them. "Why, thank you, Erik. What a nice idea." To Big Darrell she said, "I remember when you built this porch, you and Dan. You used to be quite the handyman."

Big Darrell said slowly, "I guess there's a lot of things I used to do." He looked at Erik. "Maybe I just wanted a boy to do 'em with."

"I'm ready if you are," said Erik.

Go Fish!

GOFISH

CYNTHIA DeFELICE

What did you want to be when you grew up?
Happy. That was it. No further ambitions.

When did you realize you wanted to be a writer?
Not until I was 36. Talk about late bloomers! I was working as a school librarian, which I loved, when I suddenly KNEW I wanted to try to write the kinds of books I loved sharing with my students.

What's your first childhood memory?
I was playing down in the cellar window hole of our house (don't ask me why) and I poked my head up out of the hole into the sunshine. There were buttercups growing nearby and they were very yellow in the sun. I had the clear thought that I was me, a unique person, and that I was part of the world. I was very young, probably four. I don't think I had words then for the feeling I had, but I felt its meaning very strongly.

What's your most embarrassing childhood memory?
Oooh, lots of those! And the worst part was, I couldn't hide it.
My face turned beet red—a dead giveaway every time.

What's your favorite childhood memory?
Fishing and acting as first mate on Captain Hank Garback's
charter boat with my brothers.

As a young person, who did you look up to most?
My dad, who was a good listener and very understanding.

What was your worst subject in school?
Math. Shudder. I still have math anxiety.

What was your best subject in school?
Surprise—English!

What was your first job?
Working in a bookstore in high school.

How did you celebrate publishing your first book?
Oh, I worked the celebrating to death! We celebrated the
acceptance phone call. Then the contract. Then the advance
check. The first galleys. The first review. Publication. And on
and on. Champagne, ice cream, you name it!

Where do you write your books?
In my office, second floor of my house on Seneca Lake. I am
deeply attached to my office and find it difficult to write anywhere else.

Which of your characters is most like you?
Allie Nichols from my Ghost Mysteries series—except that she is much braver, smarter, and cooler than I ever was!

When you finish a book, who reads it first?
My husband. He's a good critic. And I love getting the male point of view.

Are you a morning person or a night owl?
I'm a morning person for sure. I go to bed pathetically early.

What's your idea of the best meal ever?
Shrimp or fish pulled fresh from the ocean and cooked right then on the grill on the boat.

Which do you like better: cats or dogs?
No contest: dogs. I really enjoyed writing about Hoover, Mr. Henry's golden retriever, in the books about Allie Nichols.

What do you value most in your friends?
Humor, brains, and honesty.

Who is your favorite fictional character?
I first read *To Kill a Mockingbird* when I was in fifth grade, and Boo Radley still haunts me.

What are you most afraid of?
Giving a dumb answer to a question like this one.

What time of year do you like best?
Fall, because that's when we go on our summer vacation!

What's your favorite TV show?
NFL football.

What's the best advice you have ever received about writing?
Plan on throwing out most of what you write.

What do you want readers to remember about your books?
The characters.

What would you do if you ever stopped writing?
I hope to work with horses or dogs, and volunteer to teach adults to read.

Where in the world do you feel most at home?
I crave being outdoors.

What do you wish you could do better?
I would love to be able to play a musical instrument well, and I'd love to be an accomplished horsewoman. These are both VERY distant goals. So distant that I think I'll need to wait for my next life.

Owen McGuire is having a lonely summer.
Since his mother died, he and his father have barely talked.
Then he meets a new friend, Campion, who claims she's from a planet
called Home—she even asks Owen to come back with her.
Is she crazy? Or is she telling the truth?

Is there a better place out there somewhere?

SigNAL

CYNTHIA DeFELICE

Find out in . . .

SigNAL

1

"If I were an animal, what kind would I be? Well, that's a really interesting question, Josie. I have a lot of favorites. Obviously, no animal is nobler than the dog."

Josie, who is running ahead of me, glances back and gives me a knowing look.

"But I think I'd be a falcon. They can dive at speeds up to two hundred miles an hour. How cool would that be? Falcons fly and hunt wherever they please. They *rule* the sky."

Josie gives a yip and takes off after a squirrel. Okay, I admit it, Josie's my dog. I'm talking to my dog. Maybe it's pathetic, but I don't have anyone else to talk to.

And Josie's terrific company, let me make that clear. I have great respect for dogs in general and Josie in particular. We got her when I was five, and she's always been my best friend. Since we moved here when school ended in June, she's my only friend.

Here is upstate New York, in what everybody calls the Finger Lakes region. That's because there are eleven long, narrow lakes that look like skinny fingers. Most of them have Iroquois Indian names, like Seneca, Canandaigua, Keuka, and Cayuga. I can't remember them all.

The lakes were made by glaciers during the Ice Age, but there's an Iroquois legend that says they were formed when the Great Spirit reached down and pressed his hands into the earth. Which is kind of cool to think about, except I can't help wondering if there's another legend that explains why the Great Spirit had eleven fingers.

I like to picture those giant hands reaching down from the sky. In my mind, they're always hairy, with five fingers on one hand and six on the other.

Anyway, I'm not saying I was Mr. Popularity at my old school, but I had buddies. I miss Kevin Bowen the most. He and I did practically everything together. We were known as "Owen and Bowen." I'm Owen, obviously. Owen McGuire.

Take it from me, you don't want to move at the end of the school year. Because then there you are in a new place where you don't know anybody, and you've got the whole summer ahead of you.

We only moved a few hours away, but it feels really different here. In Buffalo, our house was in a neighborhood with a lot of kids. But now we live in what you'd have to call the boonies. There's Seneca Lake to the east, the highway to the west, and everywhere else, nothing but woods and farm fields. I like living in the country and seeing all the deer and turkeys and woodchucks, but it would be nice to see some people, too. Especially another twelve-year-old kid.

When we first got here at the end of June, I rode around on my bike to check things out. That's when I discovered the trail I'm running on now. It's seven miles long, and follows the path of a stream that runs between our lake, Seneca, and Keuka Lake. The stream has cut steep cliffs through the woods, and it's cool and shady down there. That makes it a perfect place for running, which I'm doing every day. The school I'll be going to in the fall has a soccer team for grades seven and eight, and I plan to be on it. I decided I might as well use this long summer on my own to get in shape and practice my footwork.

So Josie and I have been running every day for three and a half weeks, going about three miles up the trail and three miles back, sometimes even more. We've seen a lot of amazing stuff. Like one day Josie came toward me howling like a crazy thing, chasing a wild turkey. It flew down the trail right at me, madly flapping its wings, and just missed the top of my head. I could feel the rush of air from its wings in my hair.

Another day a black bear was standing in the trail ahead of us. Josie and I both stopped dead in our tracks.

We looked at the bear, and the bear looked at us. I glanced down at Josie, and every hair on her body was standing out so stiffly she looked a lot bigger than her normal size.

"Easy, girl," I murmured. She gave a funny little growl, and the bear ambled away. It didn't seem to want anything to do with us, but we headed back the way we had come, just in case.

Then, two days ago, Josie ran ahead and started barking at something on the path. I nearly had a heart attack when I saw it was a snapping turtle as big as home plate. Josie was dancing all around it, lunging in and out, yipping with excitement.

"No, Josie!" I cried, but she didn't stop. "Josie! If that thing clamps its jaws onto your nose, you are going to be very sorry!" I warned.

Finally, I was able to grab her collar and drag her away, but I could tell she wanted to go back there in the worst way. There are some things she's not real smart about.

I don't know the names of every single tree and plant and bird and animal we've been seeing on our runs, but I know a lot of them. When I was little, my mom gave me a set of field guides. She and Josie and I used to take long walks, and when we got home, we'd look up everything we'd seen in the books. I have guides on birds, mammals, reptiles and amphibians, wildflowers, rocks and fossils, insects, and stars. The one on stars and planets is my favorite. It was Mom's, too.

It was Mom who really taught me to notice things. So I keep my eyes open on my runs with Josie. I recognize the teeny heart-shaped tracks of fawns and the handlike prints of raccoons. By now I know the squawk of the great blue heron that we scare out of its favorite minnow-hunting spot, and the musky smell foxes leave behind. I like to look for trout and suckers in the pools of the stream, and Josie keys me in to every squirrel, rabbit, and woodchuck we pass by.

When you're running along through all that nature, it's easy to see how everything belongs. Every animal and plant has its place in the big picture. So things that *don't* belong really stand out, like a soda bottle, or candy bar wrapper, or a deflated Mylar party balloon. It ticks me off that people throw stuff like that around, and I've made it my mission to pick up trash I see and carry it out if I can.

Up ahead, I see something white lying off the path near a patch of raspberry bushes. Josie goes over to it, sniffs, then picks it up and runs along with it in her mouth.

"Josie, come!" I shout. She's always finding stinky dead animals and scraps of food people have left behind, stuff she thinks is wonderful. This looks like a paper towel or a napkin, maybe. At least it doesn't look like anything too disgusting, not that that would have stopped Josie.

She comes and I say, "Sit, Josie. Drop it." Josie is a German shorthaired pointer, a hunting dog, so she's supposed to surrender whatever she retrieves to me, her owner, the mighty hunter.

Amazingly, she sits at my first command and drops what I see now is a piece of white cloth.

"Good dog!"

There's red stuff on it. I start to pick it up, wondering what the red is. Paint?

Whoa. Gross. Quickly, I throw it back to the ground. The red stuff is, I'm pretty sure, blood. The cloth is soft and stretchy, and has a ragged edge. It looks like it was torn off the bottom of somebody's T-shirt.

Yuck. I'm not carrying *that* out, never mind my good intentions about trash removal.

I start running again. Being on the trail makes me think of all the outdoor things Mom and I used to do together. I remember a clear winter night when I was eight years old. Dad was working late. Mom got me all bundled up in my snowsuit and hat and mittens and boots, and we went outside and lay down on our backs in the snow and stared up at the sky. I barely even felt the cold because I was really noticing for the first time how enormous the sky is.

Mom told me how far away the stars are and I couldn't believe it. I asked, "Where does it *end*?" Mom said she didn't know. I kept trying to picture where the universe stopped, but I couldn't do it. You can't picture *nothing*, because as soon as you do, it's *something*.

Then Mom said, "There are eight hundred thousand galaxies and billions of stars and planets out there. I like to imagine that one of them is the sun in a solar system similar to ours."

I liked imagining it, too.

When we finally got cold and went inside, we read in the field guide to stars and planets that the number of stars is so huge that "the statistical possibility of other solar systems definitely exists." I memorized that sentence. The book also said that telescopes have shown that there are millions of galaxies beyond ours.

Mom said, "Nobody knows exactly what happened to create the Earth's solar system, Owen. But I don't see any reason to think it happened only once. It's such a small view of things, don't you agree?"

I did. I certainly didn't want to be the kind of person who had a small view of things. To me, it was logical to think there would be life beyond our one little planet. Actually, it seemed crazy to think there *wouldn't* be.

After that night, I read everything I could about space, spaceships, space travel, people's accounts of their encounters with aliens, you name it. I became convinced that not only is there life on other planets, but that they've been trying to contact us. Mom thought so, too.

Thinking about Mom is making me miss her, so I take a pretend head shot and resume my conversation with Josie. "Yes, Josie, you're right. I learned all my cool soccer moves from Dad. You know the goal we have set up in the yard where we practice taking shots after dinner? I'm getting pretty good, don't you think? I can't wait for our trip to Alaska in August. Yeah, you can come, too. Didn't we take you along when we camped in the Rockies and went fishing in the Everglades?"

Josie sniffs when I say this. She knows it's all a lie. Dad and I never go on cool trips together. There's no soccer goal in our yard. I'm just learning to play, and Dad doesn't. Play, I mean. Not soccer, not anything. Today is Sunday, and where is Dad? At work. He's always been the World's Most Dedicated Accountant, but it seems to me he started working even more after Mom died.

It was a car accident. A snowy January night a year and a half ago. She skidded into a tree on her way back from work. I was home when it happened, watching the storm out the window, urging the snow to come down faster and heavier so school would be canceled.

I don't even remember if it was or not.

For Dad and me, a huge, jagged hole suddenly opened up in our lives. We just tiptoed around it, as if maybe it would go away if we pretended hard enough.

It didn't go away. It just got bigger and deeper.

Dad and I don't talk about it. It's just the way it is.

I don't want to think about all that, and besides, Josie has gone racing ahead—too far ahead. She's really fast. For every mile I go, I bet she does five or six. She needs the exercise. As long as she gets a nice, long run every day, she's what I'm sure anyone would agree is the perfect dog. She's good even if she has to be cooped up for a couple days, but it's hard for her.

I can relate. After all, I've told her, I have to go to school.

I whistle and she comes back—with another scrap of the same T-shirt-like material in her mouth. It has a smear of bright red blood on it. When blood is still red instead of brown, it's, like, *fresh*, right?

I look around uneasily, but there's nobody else in sight. This is starting to freak me out. Let's face it; blood is creepy stuff.

Josie has taken off again, and I shrug and follow her. I wonder if it's a person or an animal that's bleeding and then realize it's a stupid question: animals don't rip up their T-shirts to blot their cuts. Probably somebody sneezed and got a bloody nose, or got scratched while picking raspberries. But what if it's something worse? I wonder if I should get help.

When we moved and it looked like I was going to be on my own for most of the summer, Dad gave me a cell phone. I could call him now. Or 911. But is this an emergency? I'm not sure. I take the phone from my pocket and turn it on. No reception. It must be because of the high cliffs on both sides of the stream.

I put the phone away and scan the ground. The trail is soft and moist here and I see footprints. Feeling like a real tracker, I stop to study them. They have the pattern of sneakers or running shoes, like the ones I'm wearing, but since they're only partial prints I can't get a sense of the size. Josie comes over and examines them, too, but doesn't seem to find them very interesting. They're not animal tracks, after all.

Then I notice that the person who made the prints has left the trail. There is an old, dilapidated mill ahead on the left. On the right is a meadow of tall grass, and it's clear someone has recently moved through it. I follow the path of broken, mashed-down stalks of grass, wondering what in the world I'm doing, but doing it anyway.

Josie apparently thinks this detour from the trail is great fun, because she bounds ahead of me, making her own path through the undergrowth. The meadow ends at a steep shale slope, and I can see an avalanche of thin, crumbly stones that were sent cascading down it by the person ahead of me, who I'm beginning to think of as "the bloody guy."

So I climb the slope, too, annoyed by the ease with which Josie manages the slippery shale incline that has me on all fours, panting and clutching at anything that looks solid. It's like climbing a sand dune, so with each step I slide back half a step.

When I get to the top of the hill, I see a house that seems to be abandoned. There are no cars, and the grass is overgrown. Beyond the house is a cornfield, a monster cornfield, and alongside that is an equally huge wheat field. Both of them stretch as far as I can see into the distance.

The guy's tracks lead right to the edge of the corn.

It's late July and we've had a lot of rain, and the cornstalks are already higher than the top of my head. They are planted right up to the edge of the yard, crowding the house, standing in silent rows and shimmering in the hushed, hot, humid air. I stand at the edge of the field where the bloody guy went in, wondering if I should bother to follow him.

I take a few steps into the corn, and that's all it takes to feel as if I've been transported to an entirely different world. The plants are so high and so thick that things look the same in every direction. I feel *swallowed up* by the corn. I fight back a panicky claustrophobia and realize that I'd never be able to find the bloody guy in here if he didn't want me to—and it's pretty obvious he *doesn't* want me to, since he seems to be purposely hiding from me.

I want to get out of that cornfield as fast as I can. I'm about to turn and retrace my steps when I hear a sound coming from out of the greenness growing all around me. I cock my head and listen closely. There it is again. Breathing. Hard breathing.

The bloody guy *is* in the corn, and not far away. He has to know I'm here, and yet he isn't saying hello or asking for help. He's hiding. And panting.

A breeze stirs the corn. The tops sigh gently, and the lower, more dried-out leaves make a clacking sound against each other. Suddenly I'm more spooked than I've ever been in my life. I turn and run out into the open air and across the farmyard. "Josie! Come!" I call. I slip and slide down that shale cliff, land at the bottom in a tangle of limbs and loose rock, then get up and run, run, run back down the trail, wanting nothing but to put distance between me and whoever is breathing out there in the corn.

Embark on new adventures
with these exciting SQUARE FISH titles

**The Girl Who
Circumnavigated
Fairyland**
Catherynne M. Valente
Illustrations by Ana Juan
ISBN 978-1-250-01019-3

Time Cat
Lloyd Alexander
ISBN 978-0-312-63213-7

The Little Secret
Kate Saunders
ISBN 978-0-312-67427-4

The Kneebone Boy
Ellen Potter
ISBN 978-0-312-67432-8

A Wrinkle in Time
Madeleine L'Engle
ISBN 978-1-250-00467-3

**The Secret
of Zoom**
Lynne Jonell
ISBN 978-0-312-65933-2

SQUARE FISH   mackids.com

Read the Allie Nichols Ghost Mysteries
AVAILABLE FROM SQUARE FISH

The Ghost of Fossil Glen • 978-0-312-60213-0

A murdered girl is sending messages to Allie,
asking to have her death avenged.
Is Allie brave enough to confront a killer?

The Ghost and Mrs. Hobbs • 978-0-312-62909-0

Allie is being haunted by a handsome
young man who needs her help dealing with
a dangerous person. Or is he the dangerous one?

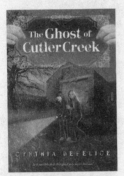

The Ghost of Cutler Creek • 978-0-312-62967-0

Another ghost is trying to contact Allie,
but how can she help a ghost who won't speak?
Is it possible this ghost was never human?

The Ghost of Poplar Point • 978-0-374-32540-4

A ghost is haunting Allie's dreams with
frightening scenes. But if Allie tries to
help this ghost, she could risk destroying
her entire town.